Captain Stone's
Revenge

Read all the mysteries in the
NANCY DREW DIARIES

Nancy Drew
DIARIES™

Captain Stone's Revenge

#24

CAROLYN KEENE

Aladdin
NEW YORK LONDON TORONTO SYDNEY NEW DELHI

ALADDIN

An imprint of Simon & Schuster Children's Publishing Division

1230 Avenue of the Americas, New York, New York 10020

First Aladdin paperback edition January 2023

Text copyright © 2023 by Simon & Schuster, Inc.

Cover illustration copyright © 2023 by Erin McGuire

Also available in an Aladdin hardcover edition.

All rights reserved, including the right of reproduction in whole or in part in any form.

ALADDIN and related logo are registered trademarks of Simon & Schuster, Inc.

NANCY DREW, NANCY DREW DIARIES, and colophons are registered trademarks of Simon & Schuster, Inc.

For information about special discounts for bulk purchases, please contact Simon & Schuster Special Sales at 1-866-506-1949 or business@simonandschuster.com.

The Simon & Schuster Speakers Bureau can bring authors to your live event. For more information or to book an event contact the Simon & Schuster Speakers Bureau at 1-866-248-3049 or visit our website at www.simonspeakers.com.

Series designed by Karin Paprocki

Cover designed by Alicia Mikles

Interior designed by Mike Rosamilia

The text of this book was set in Adobe Caslon Pro.

Manufactured in the United States of America 1222 OFF

2 4 6 8 10 9 7 5 3 1

Library of Congress Cataloging-in-Publication Data

Names: Keene, Carolyn, author.

Title: Captain Stone's revenge / Carolyn Keene.

Description: First Aladdin paperback edition. | New York : Aladdin, 2023. | Series: Nancy Drew diaries ; 24 | Audience: Ages 8 to 12. | Summary: Nancy investigates a string of incidents at a sailing resort.

Identifiers: LCCN 2022012409 (print) | LCCN 2022012410 (ebook) | ISBN 9781534469426 (paperback) | ISBN 9781534469433 (hardcover) | ISBN 9781534469440 (ebook)

Subjects: CYAC: Resorts—Fiction. | Sailing—Fiction. | Mystery and detective stories. | LCGFT: Detective and mystery fiction.

Classification: LCC PZ7.K23 Carh 2023 (print) | LCC PZ7.K23 (ebook) | DDC [Fic]—dc23

LC record available at https://lccn.loc.gov/2022012409

LC ebook record available at https://lccn.loc.gov/2022012410

Contents

Captain Stone's
Revenge

Dear Diary,

I'M SO EXCITED! BESS, GEORGE, AND I are headed to Vermont to visit my family friend Megan Cho. Megan is opening an eco-resort and sailing club on beautiful Lake Champlain, and she invited us to spend a few days with her and attend the grand opening! I can't wait. We're going to sail, hike, and relax by the lake. I promised Bess and George this would be a real vacation—no mysteries. Okay, I said I'd do my best to make it a real vacation. After all, I don't like to make promises I'm not sure I can keep. . . .

CHAPTER ONE

Mystery with a Side of Maple Syrup

THE AIRPLANE MADE A WIDE TURN AS IT descended through the clouds toward Burlington International Airport. I pressed my face against the small oval window. All at once, I could see green hills, fields dotted with farms, and our ultimate destination: the clear blue waters of Lake Champlain.

"We're almost there!" I said. It was my first trip to Vermont, one of the smallest and least populated states in the country. I couldn't wait to explore, try the world-famous maple syrup, and of course, go sailing at my friend Megan's new club and resort!

"Thank goodness!" George grumbled behind me. Our small commercial jet's seats were grouped in twos. George had taken the seat behind me and Bess. She was using the empty space next to her to stash her computer, e-reader, and cell phone.

"Motion sickness?" Bess asked, dabbing on fresh lip gloss in preparation for landing.

"No, my e-reader is about to run out of charge!" George said with a groan. "And I'm right in the middle of a really good book! What sort of airplane doesn't have power outlets?"

"Maybe the kind that's built to fly, not charge all your equipment? I mean, I know which one I'd prefer," I teased. George gave my seat a little nudge and we laughed.

Bess put the cap on her lip gloss and dropped it into her navy-blue purse. As usual, her outfit was perfectly themed for our destination. She wore a blue-and-white-striped shirt with a sailboat crest on the front, white linen pants, and a pair of navy Top-Siders. Her cousin George, on the other hand, was outfitted in cargo pants with enough pockets to hold all her electronics. (I don't even want to talk about how long it took us to get through security back in River Heights!)

The intercom dinged and the captain came on. "Hello, passengers," she said in a smooth voice. "We're making our final descent into Burlington, where skies are clear and the temperature is seventy-five degrees on this beautiful June day. In preparation for landing, please return your seat backs and tray tables to their upright positions. We'll be on the ground shortly!"

I folded the Sudoku puzzle I'd been working on, tucked it away, and clicked my tray table back into place. I sat up straight. The plane took a sharp turn and descended quickly, angling toward the runway. In a matter of minutes, the wheels touched down with a thump. We lurched forward in our seats as the plane slowed. I pulled out my phone and switched it off airplane mode. A text notification immediately filled the screen. It was from Megan.

Nancy! I'm so sorry, but I'll be late picking you up. Had a little accident this morning. Nothing major! Will explain when I get there. Can't wait to see you all!

Poor Megan! I wondered what happened. I told Bess and George about the delay, then quickly texted Megan back to let her know it was no problem, of course, and we hoped everything was okay. I never minded having a little time to explore, anyway. There's always something new to see and learn, wherever you go.

The plane rolled to a stop in front of the gate and the seat-belt light clicked off. George, Bess, and I stood and grabbed our luggage from the overhead compartments. We followed the line of passengers off the plane.

"We have a little time to kill," I said once we were inside the small airport. "What would you like to do?"

"Hmmm . . . ," Bess said, glancing around. "I'm not sure. Is there a gift shop somewhere?"

"Gift shop? No thanks," George said. She was already following her nose toward a gate-side restaurant called the Skinny Pancake.

"You're hungry again already?" Bess asked as we

caught up with George. "We just ate two hours ago at the airport in River Heights."

"Exactly," George said. "It's been two whole hours! And they didn't even have pretzels on our flight. I'm starving! Besides, how big can a skinny pancake be?"

Bess and I laughed. George is basically a bottomless pit when it comes to food. She's like her e-reader. Always needing to be charged.

We dragged our luggage to the restaurant, stepped up to the counter, and read the extensive menu written above the register on a large chalkboard.

"Wow," Bess said, scanning the board. "Who knew there were so many ways to eat a crepe? Strawberries . . . egg and bacon . . . ham and cheese. How am I supposed to choose?"

"We could always get one of everything!" George volunteered.

"That would be, like, twenty crepes!" I said with a laugh.

"And?" George answered with a smirk. "Is that a problem?"

A middle-aged woman with long, shiny hair pulled into a ponytail stepped up to the register. "Good afternoon!" she said brightly. Her name tag read ELSIE. "What can I get for you?"

"Ah, it's so hard to choose," I said. "What do you recommend?"

"Depends," Elsie answered. "Do you want sweet or savory?"

"Yes!" George responded, and we all cracked up.

After a few moments of deliberation, we placed our orders. Elsie typed them into the computer. "Great choices," she said. Of course, I wasn't sure there were any *bad* choices here. "Can I interest you all in a maple latte to go with your crepes?"

Bess's eyes widened. "A *maple* latte? I didn't even know that was a thing!"

"Oh, it's a thing." Elsie smiled. "A very delicious thing."

"We'll take three, right?" I said. Bess and George nodded.

A gate announcement sounded over the intercom

as another plane arrived. Soon after, a few more passengers filtered into the restaurant, stepping in line behind us. I paid. Elsie handed me a table stand with a number 7 on top.

"Have a seat," she said. "I'll bring out your food when it's ready."

"Thank you," I said.

Bess, George, and I chose a table close to the window, where we could watch the planes taking off and landing. Some people hate airports. Not me. I kind of love them. I enjoy all the coming and going. The possibilities are infinite, right? It's a bit like solving a mystery. The journey could take you just about anywhere.

Elsie came over holding a tray full of mugs.

"So, are you arriving or departing?" she asked.

"Just arrived," I answered.

"And what brings you to the Green Mountain State?" Elsie asked, placing steaming lattes with maple leaves etched in the foam at each of our places. Bess already had her mug to her lips before I could open my mouth to answer Elsie's question.

"We're visiting my friend," I said. "Megan Cho? She's opening an eco-resort and sailing club by the Gemstone Islands."

"Ah, I'd heard someone had bought that old property and was rebuilding the resort," Elsie answered. "Exciting!"

"So you know the place?" I asked.

Elsie cleared her throat. "Sure do," she said. "Pretty famous around these parts. Nearly everyone of a certain age has memories of the old Gemstone Islands Resort. Had my senior prom there. Quite a time! The old resort was rumored to be haunted, you know," she said with a wink.

"Haunted?" Bess's eyebrows quirked up.

"That's what people say," Elsie answered. "Should have seen the looks on everyone's faces at my prom when the power suddenly flicked off for two minutes. Never heard anything louder in my life than that shriek Jennifer Hutchins, our prom queen, let out." Elsie laughed at the memory. "And when the lights came back on, one of the guys had put on this old pirate's hat from a display in the dining room and jumped out at everyone. Jennifer screamed even louder!"

Elsie chuckled, and then her face went dark. "Of course, all that haunting talk wasn't so funny ten years later when, well . . ." She paused and cleared her throat again.

"When what?" George asked.

Bess lowered her latte mug, a dollop of steamed milk clinging to her nose. She wiped it away with a sheepish grin, staring intently at Elsie.

"Oh, it's nothing," Elsie answered. She shuddered slightly, then pasted a big smile on her face. "Nothing to worry about now, I'm sure! That was a long time ago. It's not like the place is *actually* haunted. You know how people like to talk," she said, a bit too brightly. Then she cocked her head as if she'd just heard something. "Oh, pardon me! I think that was the bell. Your crepes must be up." She hurried away, green apron swishing against her legs.

"Huh, I didn't hear anything, did you?" Bess said.

George shook her head.

"Interesting . . ." I turned and watched Elsie, who was standing at the very obviously empty counter between the seating area and the kitchen. Our crepes were definitely not up. There was a familiar tingle on the back of my neck. Call it my detective radar. I took a long sip of my latte, thinking.

"Oh no," Bess said, shaking her head. "Really?"

George rolled her eyes. "Just one vacation, Nancy? One! Do you think we could have one trip without a mystery? You promised!"

I set my latte mug down on the table.

"Technically, I said I'd try. I can't help it if intrigue follows me everywhere I go. Besides," I added with a grin, "I thought that's why you liked to hang out with me. It's never boring, right?"

"Hmm, I don't know about that. I'm just in it for the maple lattes," Bess answered with a grin of her own. She slurped down the rest of her drink in one fantastic gulp. "That was delicious! Would it be bad to have one more?"

"Only if you want to spend the rest of the afternoon

bouncing off the walls," George said. "I've seen you after two cups of coffee, remember?"

"Ah," Bess said with a sigh. "Water it is, then."

A few minutes later, a bell actually did sound in the kitchen. The chef slid three plates across the counter. Elsie picked them up, flawlessly juggling all three on her left arm. She weaved through the tables and set the crepes and a silver container of maple syrup in front of us.

"Enjoy!" she said, before dashing off to help a weary group of travelers with rumpled hair and clothes who had slumped their way to the counter.

George speared a banana chunk covered in chocolate and fresh whipped cream and popped it into her mouth.

"Mmmmm," she said, eyes closed. "Chocolate and banana. Nothing better!"

Bess and I dug in, savoring our mouthwatering crepes. Mine was filled with eggs and Vermont cheddar. Bess's was smeared with hazelnut spread and strawberries. She still dumped half the container of syrup on it anyway. I sometimes wonder if the reason Bess is so sweet is that she's 99 percent composed of sugar.

"What do you suppose Elsie meant about the old resort being haunted?" I said, taking another bite of delicious crepe.

"Are you still thinking about that?" George asked.

"Of course she is," Bess said. "She's Nancy Drew! Famous amateur sleuth. She can't help herself!"

"I'm just curious," I said. "That's all."

Curiosity is an itch. If I don't scratch, all it does is itch even more. I continued to chew and think, gazing absentmindedly out the window at the planes taxiing on the runway. I figured Elsie was probably in her forties. So whatever happened at the resort must have been around fifteen to twenty years ago. Weird that it still made her seem so . . . *jumpy*.

"Earth to Nancy. . . ." George waved her fork in front of my face. "Are you done?"

"Oh!" I snapped my attention back to the table. Elsie had returned and was motioning toward our plates.

"Looks like you enjoyed your lunch?" she said.

"Yes, it was fabulous!" Bess said.

"Can I clear your dishes?" Elsie asked.

"Yes, thank you," I answered.

"Thank you, too!" she said. "I hope you enjoy your visit!"

She stacked our plates and turned to leave. I was just about to stop her—I *really* wanted to ask her more about the old Gemstone Islands Resort and ghost rumors. But my phone buzzed before I could open my mouth and speak. I checked my messages.

"Megan is out front!"

"Phew! Saved by the bell," Bess said. "Time to forget you heard anything about a ghost, okay?"

"Ha-ha," I answered. We gathered our things and exited the airport, stepping into the fresh Vermont air. Megan was parked at the curb, standing next to a red Mini Cooper and waving.

More like, Megan was *leaning* on her Mini Cooper, waving—and wincing a little. All her weight was on her right foot.

Her left foot was wrapped in a brown elastic bandage and stuffed into a huge black stabilizing boot.

CHAPTER TWO

❧

The Sail Away

"NANCY!" MEGAN SAID. "WELCOME! IT'S SO great to see you."

I hurried over and gave her a big hug. "It's so great to see you, too." I pulled back. "What happened to your foot, though? Is that from the accident you texted about?"

"Yep." She sighed. "I was out walking Jimmy Chew on the trails by the resort this morning and stepped right into a hole some animal must have dug. Can you believe it? Four days before my grand opening. My timing is awful! Had to get an X-ray and everything.

At least it's just a sprain. I'll be stuck in this boot for a few weeks, but it could have been worse. Anyway, sorry I'm late!"

"It's no problem," I said. "I'm sorry you got hurt!"

I introduced Bess and George.

"Nice to finally meet you," Megan said, extending a hand. "I've heard so much about both of you over the years when Nancy and her dad visited my family in Brooklyn."

Megan is in her mid-thirties. Even though we don't get to see each other a lot, she's always been like a cool young aunt to me. Our families have been friends forever. Her dad was my dad's adviser back in law school. Megan followed in her father's footsteps and became a lawyer too. Her specialty is environmental law. She won a huge case a couple of years ago against a boat tour company that was polluting the Hudson River with toxic chemicals. So she decided to take the proceeds and open her own environmentally friendly resort and sailing club. Of course, that meant leaving the city—where she'd spent her entire life—and moving to rural Vermont.

"We've heard all about you, too," George said. "Thanks for having us!"

Bess nodded. "Yes, thank you! And I'm really sorry about your foot."

"Oh, it's fine," Megan said. "Hurt my pride more than anything. I was pretty good at avoiding open manhole covers back in Brooklyn. I wasn't prepared for the animal hole or whatever it was I stepped in today. Thank goodness my neighbor's grandson happened to be nearby. He took Jimmy Chew's leash and helped me hobble back to the house. But enough of that! At least it's my left foot and I can still drive. Hop on in. I can't wait to show you around the new property!"

After stowing our luggage in the trunk, George, Bess, and I squished into Megan's car. And I mean we *squished*. Megan's Mini definitely lived up to its name. There was barely enough room for all of us. Bess and George squeezed into the tiny back seat. I climbed in front and pulled the seat forward until my knees were pressed against the glove compartment so that George and Bess would have more space.

"Sorry, I know it's small," Megan said. "But it's electric. As you know, I'm committed to preserving the environment. There was no way I'd let my first car be a gas guzzler."

"This is your first car?" George piped up from the back seat.

"Yep," Megan said. "Never had a need for one in the city. I took public transportation everywhere. Obviously that's not an option here."

Megan stepped on the accelerator and the car quietly pulled onto the road. We exited the airport, hopped on the highway, and headed north. Soon the clusters of houses and buildings that surrounded the airport yielded to majestic trees and rolling fields. Black-and-white cows grazed alongside red-painted barns. Corn and other produce grew in neatly planted rows.

"Farming is still a huge part of rural life here," Megan said. "Sadly, many of the area's small family farms struggle to survive. That's why I'm going to use fresh farm-to-table produce at the resort whenever I can. Not only is it the right thing to do to support local farmers, but it also cuts down on emissions from shipping goods cross-country."

Megan hit the turn signal and we exited the highway. After a few more scenic miles, we reached a small village. The sign at the edge read: WELCOME TO BURNHAM, HOME OF THE GEMSTONE ISLANDS!

The Burnham village center featured a small square that was surrounded by a white-steepled church, brick town offices, and a row of Victorian houses. A white-painted gazebo sat in the center of the square.

"This place is adorable!" Bess squealed from the back seat.

Megan smiled. "It is. They hold band concerts in that gazebo every Friday in the summer," she said. "People bring picnics and blankets and sit on the green and listen. It's a lot of fun."

"Sounds like it." I was happy to see how much Megan was already enjoying her adopted hometown.

Even though she had always loved nature, moving from the city to the country was a big change.

We headed away from the village and turned down a narrow road that curved between tall trees on one side and a steep rock ledge on the other. Megan's car hugged the side of the road tightly as she drove. A bicyclist whizzed by in the other direction, taking up the entire opposite lane. I couldn't imagine what would happen if another car happened to come at the same time too.

"Wow, I can see why you'd want a small car," I said. "And not just for environmental reasons!"

Megan laughed. "Yes, not much room for error out here, that's for sure!"

We rounded another corner, and the sparkling blue waters of Lake Champlain flickered in and out of view between the trees on our left. The lake was dotted with all sorts of boats: sailboats, fishing boats, speedboats pulling kids on tubes. In the distance, I could make out the silhouette of a jagged mountain range.

"Those are the Adirondacks," Megan explained.

"You can see the most beautiful sunsets over them from my front porch. Never gets old!"

The car crested a steep hill. From up here, I could see we were actually on a peninsula, surrounded by Lake Champlain on three sides. As we drove down the hill, we passed a field of wildflowers swaying in the breeze to the right. On the other side, another tree-covered hill blocked the lake view. Megan pointed at the hill.

"That's where I twisted my ankle," she said. "Hiking up at Pirate's Perch. Beautiful view up there, but you'd better watch your step!"

"Good thing I'd rather shop than hike!" Bess said. We laughed.

Finally, the car reached a tree-lined gravel driveway. A hand-painted sign was posted at the end: GEMSTONE ISLANDS ECO-RESORT AND SAILING CLUB.

We turned. The narrow driveway threaded its way through the tall trees until it opened up to a beautiful lakeside property situated on a small cove. There were two Cape Cod–style buildings facing the water, one large and one small. Both sported gray shingles and crisp white trim and had colorful flowerpots lining the front steps. Megan explained that the larger building, on the right, was the guest lodge and club. The smaller cottage to the left was her private residence. George, Bess, and I would be staying with her in the cottage while the finishing touches were put on the lodge.

Megan parked and hobbled from the car, beckoning us to follow. We got out and grabbed our suitcases, then traipsed up the crushed stone walkway behind Megan. I sucked in a deep breath of warm air. It smelled like freshly cut grass and sunshine.

"It's beautiful here," I said.

"It sure is!" Bess agreed. George nodded.

"Thank you!" Megan said. "It's been a lot of work. This place was in ruins and completely overgrown when I bought it. But it's been totally worth the effort! I was able to build off the foundation of the old resort, but on a smaller scale and more environmentally friendly."

"Is that why you call it an eco-resort?" George asked.

"Yes," Megan answered. "That's one of the reasons. Every decision I made was based on reducing the property's environmental impact. We have geothermal heating and cooling, solar power, and a rainwater-fed irrigation system. I was also able to salvage some brick and marble from the old resort, which I incorporated into the lodge's fireplace."

"That's amazing." I cast a glance toward the lodge next door. "Was the old resort abandoned or something?"

"Not exactly," Megan answered. "The old resort burned down. The property has changed hands a number of times since, but I'm the first person to actually build out here."

"How long ago did the resort burn down?" George asked.

"Oh, a long time. Fifteen years ago." Megan twisted a key in the lock and opened the cottage's front door.

I immediately thought of Elsie at the airport. Was that what she was thinking of when she stopped talking about the old resort so abruptly? Then I did my best to shove that thought from my mind. I was here to have fun with my friends—not contemplate something that had happened more than a decade ago. I'd made a sort-of promise, after all.

"Come on in," Megan said.

We followed her into a small foyer. Jimmy Chew, Megan's Jack Russell terrier, bounded around the corner and skidded to a stop on all four paws, tail wagging. Megan leaned over and rubbed his ears. Jimmy promptly flopped onto his back, paws pedaling the air, and squirmed in anticipation of belly rubs.

Megan obliged and gave him a little pat. "Okay, that's enough, Jimmy!" she said. "Let's show our guests inside."

We moved from the foyer into a living area with a panoramic view of the lake. A set of French doors opened to a covered porch. A grassy lawn extended behind the cottage and adjacent lodge, gently sloping down to a sandy beach and dock area. Three Hobie Cats with brightly colored sails and a small motorboat were tied toward the front of the dock. A regal navy-hulled sailboat bobbed gently at the end.

"This is spectacular!" I said. "I don't know what this place looked like before, but you've done an incredible job."

Bess and George nodded.

"Thanks," Megan answered. "We can leave your bags here for now and I'll give you a tour of the property. Anyone thirsty or hungry?"

George opened her mouth. Bess shot her a look and quickly shook her head.

"No, we ate at the airport," Bess said. "But thank you!"

We left our luggage in the cottage's living area and followed Megan onto the back porch, Jimmy Chew trotting behind us. The porch was decorated with a pair of blue Adirondack chairs and potted flowers in red, orange, and purple. From here, we had a great view of the dock, sailboats, and lake. I leaned on the porch railing as Megan pointed at three small tree-covered islands that sat in the water just beyond the dock.

"Those are the Gemstone Islands," Megan explained.

"They got their name because of the way they are lined up, like gems on a necklace. Nobody lives out there. But there are some interesting caves and beaver dams. We have kayaks that guests and club members will be able to use. So feel free to help yourselves and check things out!" She gestured at a half-dozen brightly painted kayaks lined up on the beachfront.

"Thank you," I said. "That sounds fun!"

"C'mon, let's continue the tour," Megan said over her shoulder as she hobbled down the steps onto the back lawn. Jimmy bounded across the grass toward a flock of geese at the water's edge. The geese took flight in a massive whoosh of feathered wings while Jimmy yapped excitedly.

We crossed the lawn to the guest lodge next door and went inside.

"Whoa," George said, looking around.

Whoa was right. The lodge was stunning. At the very center was an airy great room with a wall of windows overlooking the lake. Rough-hewn wood beams crisscrossed the high ceiling. A tall stone fireplace filled nearly the entire left wall. The room was decorated with cozy sofas, thick wood tables and chairs, and photographs of the lake. A fluffy dog bed was tucked in the corner for Jimmy. He curled up on it, resting his head on his paws with a sigh.

"This place is gorgeous!" I said.

"Thanks. This room will be the center of activity for lodge and club functions," Megan said. "We'll serve meals here, and host lectures about birding and local wildlife and such. There are five guest rooms upstairs, each outfitted with locally handcrafted furniture and art."

"You really put a lot of thought into every detail," Bess said. I could tell she was impressed. Bess loves details, especially when it comes to design and art.

A man wearing overalls and a ball cap walked into the room, carrying a paint bucket.

"Oh," he said, stopping. "Sorry to disturb you, Miss Cho! I didn't know you had visitors. Thought I was here alone today." He tugged on the rim of his cap with his free hand, eyes darting between me, George, and Bess.

"Hello, Owen," Megan said. "You're not disturbing us. Meet my guests: Nancy, George, and Bess. They'll be spending a few days here with me. Girls, meet Owen. He's helping spiff the place up for the grand opening celebration."

"Good to meet ya," Owen said. "Just have a couple of touch-ups to do, then I'll be out of your hair." He climbed a ladder by the fireplace and started painting the trim.

I wandered to a rack of glossy brochures and picked up one that read *Trail Map*.

"That's a guide to the trails around the property," Megan explained. "It's quite a network, with some amazing lake vistas, especially up at Pirate's Perch, as I mentioned. Definitely worth the hike."

"I had no idea you owned this much land out here," I said, reading the map.

"Actually, I don't," Megan answered. "I have an agreement with Charlotte Lawson, who owns the property next door. She'll allow my guests and club members to hike across her trails. In return, she and her grandson can use the resort's beach and dock. It's a good arrangement, and Charlotte is as sweet as they get. Ricky's a great kid too."

"Nice," I said. "We'll have to check out the trails."

"Definitely," Megan said. "I'll be in and out quite a bit over the next day or two, getting ready for the opening celebration. I have to meet with the caterers tomorrow morning and the tent rental company after that. It's been a ton of work getting ready, but it's going to be so much fun! We'll be having a barbecue on the back lawn, followed by a tour of the lake on the *Sail Away*. Speaking of, let me show you my pride and joy!"

Megan led us through the back door and onto the lodge's wide porch. More colorful Adirondack chairs were lined up in a row, facing the lake. The railing was decorated with turquoise, blue, and purple boat bumpers.

Megan pointed toward the sailboat tied at the end of the dock, bobbing gently in the water. The hull and mast were painted a crisp white that perfectly contrasted with the bright blue sky. The white sails had been lowered and secured.

"There she is. A classic Morris twenty-eight-footer."

Megan beamed. "I've done almost all the refurbishing myself. Including sanding, staining, and polishing the original teak deck."

"Wow, it looks brand-new!" Bess said, nodding in appreciation. "Like a postcard image."

"And great boat name too!" George added.

"Thanks! Let's check it out," Megan said.

As we traversed the lawn, the wind began to pick up. My hair whipped in front of my face. I pulled a hair tie from my wrist and wrestled the flyaway strands into a ponytail.

"I should have warned you," Megan said, tucking her own dark hair behind her ears. "It can get pretty windy out here."

"You picked the right spot for a sailing club, then," George said with a grin.

There was another strong gust, followed by an odd creaking sound. The *Sail Away* twisted in the wind. Something about the way the boat angled away from the dock didn't look quite right. Shouldn't it be tied at both ends?

There was another creak. This time, the sailboat turned completely sideways.

"Um, Megan . . . ," I started.

"Oh no!" she said, racing toward the dock as fast as her booted foot would allow. "It looks like I didn't knot the lines tight enough. I need to secure the boat before it gets damaged!"

"We'll help," I said.

Bess, George, and I ran ahead of Megan, straight toward the *Sail Away*.

But before we could reach the boat, another gust of wind caught it and pushed it free of the dock. A loose rope dangled from the bow. I leapt forward, trying to catch it, but missed.

The wind blew harder.

And the *Sail Away* began to drift. A hundred feet beyond the docks, the rocky caves surrounding the Gemstone Islands jutted from the water like jagged teeth. In a matter of minutes, the *Sail Away* would crash right into them—if we didn't get to it first.

CHAPTER THREE

A Sinister Message

"MEGAN, I'M SORRY!" I CRIED. "I TRIED TO catch it."

"It's not your fault," Megan said. She hurried to the base of the dock and flung open a locker. She pulled out four bright orange life jackets and yanked one over her head. Then she threw the others to Bess, George, and me.

"Put those on and hop in!" she shouted as she climbed into the motorboat.

My friends and I slipped the life jackets on and tightened the straps. We piled into the boat alongside

Megan. It bobbed in the water as she started the engine and untied it from the dock. I kept my eye on the sailboat, which was drifting closer and closer to the jagged rocks.

Any minute now and it would crash into them!

Just then there was the *bzzzzzzz* of another engine moving rapidly in our direction. Out of nowhere, an aluminum fishing boat appeared and zipped straight past the dock, toward the *Sail Away*. A teenage boy with wind-whipped blond hair stood at the boat's helm, one hand on the steering wheel, the other holding a rope.

He slowed and carefully steered alongside the *Sail Away*. Engine idling, he deftly hooked his rope on the sailboat's front cleat. Slowly, he began towing it back to the dock.

Megan retied the motorboat and killed the engine. We climbed out and hurried to the end of the dock. Megan handed me a pole with a hook on the end. "Use this to help pull her in and I'll work on tying the lines," she said.

Once the boy got close enough, I snagged the boat's front cleat with the hook and helped guide it to the dock. Megan quickly got to work securing the boat. When she was finished, she let out a relieved sigh.

The boy powered down his engine and idled in the water just past the dock.

"Hey, Miss Cho," he said with a little wave.

"Ricky," Megan answered, wiping a bead of sweat from her forehead. "Thank you! I don't even know what to say. When I named my boat the *Sail Away*, I didn't really intend for her to do just that!"

Ricky chuckled.

"Seriously, though," Megan said. "I can't thank you enough. That's twice today you've come to my rescue! I'm going to have to put you on the payroll soon."

"It's no problem," Ricky said. "That's what neighbors do. I was out fishing when I saw the boat drifting. I'm glad I was close by. What happened?"

"The lines snapped," Megan answered. She knelt on the dock, pulled a piece of severed rope from the cleat, and held it up. "See? Looks like something chewed right through it. Between this and stepping in the hole this morning, I guess the scorecard for today is animals: two, Megan: zero. I can't believe all the mischief the wildlife gets into around here. And I've seen a rat carry an entire bagel down a fire escape in the city!"

Ricky frowned. "I don't know. We have plenty of beavers and muskrats down here. Sometimes even a few minks. But I've never known them to chew through a line. A bit of dock, maybe. But never a line. And *both* of them?"

Megan shrugged. "Don't know what else would've done it," she said. "Anyway, where are my manners? Let me introduce you to my guests. Ricky, this is Nancy, Bess, and George. Girls, meet Ricky Sensbach. He lives in New Jersey and goes to high school there. But he spends his summers here with his grandmother, Charlotte."

Ricky waved again. "Nice to meet you. First time in Burnham?"

The three of us nodded.

"Oh!" Ricky said. "You're gonna love it. The hiking

and boating are off the charts here. And you definitely need to hit the Shack for a maple creemee."

"The where for the what?" George said.

"And did you say maple?" Bess piped up.

"The Shack," Ricky said. "It's right up the road in town. Best maple creemees in Vermont. They make 'em with their own syrup. Anyway, I've got to run. I'm a little behind on a project." His blue eyes danced with mischief. He put his boat in reverse, then slowed and shouted, "Hey, do you all like to fish?"

I looked at Bess, assuming that was who Ricky was *really* asking. Almost everywhere we go, someone winds up with a huge crush on Bess. She just has that effect on people. But Ricky wasn't looking at Bess. He was staring straight at George with a big grin on his face.

George glanced over her shoulder as if to check whether someone else was standing behind her. Then her face flared bright red. "Are you talking to me?" She ran her hand through her short black hair.

"Well, all of you," Ricky answered. "But yeah, you. Do you like to go fishing?"

"Fishing? With actual poles?" George said. "And hooks?"

"What else would you fish with?" Ricky asked, eyebrows bunched.

"I don't know," George answered. "I've only fished with a joystick on my Wii."

Ricky shrugged. "Okay. The real thing is a lot more fun. If you're interested, I know all the best spots. Trout, bass, perch, pike . . . Let me know!"

And with that, he motored away. George stood there a moment, clearly unsure what to do next. She pulled out her phone and busied herself by tapping the screen and scrolling through her Instagram feed.

"Well," Bess said, breaking the silence, "I still don't know what a creemee is. But if it has maple syrup in it, then count me in!"

Megan chuckled. "Creemees are what the locals call soft-serve ice cream," she said. "And Ricky's right. The Shack's maple creemees are to die for. We'll make sure to grab one while you're here. Sound good?"

"Yeah, that sounds awesome," I said. But I was still

gazing at the *Sail Away*. I wasn't an expert on beavers or muskrats, but I had to agree with Ricky. It didn't seem likely that an animal had chewed through the ropes.

"Uh-oh," George said, eyeballing me. "Nancy's got that look again. . . ."

"Nancy," Bess said. "You promised. . . ."

Correction, I said I'd *do my best*. Which was not the same thing as a promise. "Can I have a look at that rope?" I asked Megan.

Megan handed me the severed line. I held it in the air. "No teeth marks," I said, turning it over. "And it looks too straight to be the work of an animal chewing."

"Are you saying it was cut?" Bess asked.

"It looks possible," I said.

"On purpose?" George asked.

"I'm not sure," I answered. "Can you think of any reason someone would cut the lines, Megan?"

"Not really," she said. Her gaze drifted past me, toward the shore. A white-haired man was walking down a path alongside the lake, leaning heavily on an old wooden cane. He stopped near the dock and squinted in our direction from behind a pair of black-rimmed glasses.

"What's going on over there?" he said in a gruff voice. "Some sort of problem?"

"No problem, Mr. Plath," Megan said brightly. "The *Sail Away* came loose. It's all fine now. Looks like an animal chewed through the lines."

"Harrumph," the man said. "An animal, you say?"

"Yep, just an animal, Mr. Plath," she said. "Nothing to concern yourself with. You have a nice day!"

"Harrumph," he said again. "An animal. I don't know about that. Maybe you need to be a bit more careful with your knots."

"I know how to tie a knot," Megan said under her breath.

"Or," Mr. Plath continued, "maybe the captain doesn't want your resort down here either!"

"The captain?" I said. "Who's that?"

Megan rolled her eyes. "Long story," she said,

watching the old man walk away around the bend and out of sight. "Nothing to worry about. Sorry about Mr. Plath. He's a bit of a grump, but I'm kind of stuck with him."

"What do you mean?" George asked.

"I guess you could say he came with the property. That is, he has a deeded right-of-way across my beach," Megan said. "And he makes sure to use it. Every day. He lives right over there on the other side of the cove." She pointed at a small lakeside cabin around the corner. It was the only other residence in sight down here.

I set down the rope and walked around the side of the *Sail Away*. That little itch in my brain was getting . . . well, *itchier*. Something was off about this whole situation. I could feel it. The same way you can feel when a teacher is about to call on you in class.

I moved around to the end of the dock and inspected the *Sail Away*'s stern. That's the back end of a boat.

What I saw made me freeze in my tracks.

"Megan?" I said, swallowing hard.

"What is it, Nancy?" she asked.

"During all the commotion, I think we might have missed something," I said. "Something that would indicate this cut line wasn't the work of animals. . . ."

Megan, Bess, and George hurried over and stood alongside me. I pointed to where the boat's name, *Sail Away*, had been written in elegant navy script.

Only someone had x-ed out the word "Sail" and painted over it. So now, the boat's name read: *Stay Away*!

CHAPTER FOUR

~⚮~

The Captain's Curse

MEGAN'S HAND FLEW TO HER MOUTH. "I can't believe this!" she said. "Why would someone do such a thing?"

I'd like to say I couldn't believe it either. But I've investigated enough cases to know that people do some pretty unbelievable things at times. "I'm so sorry," I said. "Have you noticed anything—or anyone—unusual around here recently?"

Megan shook her head. "Not really," she answered. "But I've been so busy getting ready for the opening, I haven't really been focused on anything else."

"What about that guy who just walked by?" George asked.

"Mr. Plath?" Megan said.

"Yes, he didn't seem too friendly," I said. "Has he been causing you any problems?"

"He's definitely been a thorn in my side ever since I started rebuilding the resort," Megan said.

"How so?" Bess asked.

"Oh, he's filed objections to just about everything I've tried to do," Megan said. "Claimed I'd be disturbing the wetlands, disturbing the nesting egrets . . . disturbing *Mr. Plath*. I was only able to get the permits to build the resort because the foundations were already in place and he couldn't argue against those."

"Interesting," I said.

"Yeah," Megan said. "But I'm not sure sneaky vandalism is Mr. Plath's style. He has no problem being vocal about his complaints. Quite vocal."

"Except those complaints didn't work," Bess pointed out.

"True." Megan sighed. "I'd better go into town and

report this to the sheriff. I'm really sorry your vacation is getting off to such a terrible start! Please, feel free to take out the kayaks or go for a hike. Have some fun while I'm gone."

"Don't be sorry," I said. "We want to help. Do you mind if we have a look around? See if we can find any clues?"

"Have at it," Megan answered. "I'll see you in a bit."

After Megan departed, I climbed aboard the *Sail Away*. George and Bess watched from the dock.

"See anything unusual?" George asked.

Muddy footprints tracked across the sailboat's main deck. They'd been smudged by water, so it was hard to tell exactly what size or type of shoes they came from. But one thing I knew for sure—they didn't come from Megan. There was no way she'd walk across her pride and joy in a pair of muddy shoes. "Somebody was definitely on here," I said. "Recently, too, I'd say." I ran a finger through a footprint. The dirt was fairly fresh.

The footprints stopped at the back of the boat, before turning around again. I leaned over the stern and inspected the writing. The paint was a grayish blue. I sat up and looked at my friends.

"Did either of you happen to notice what color Owen was painting inside the lodge?" I asked.

"Of course," Bess said. "It was"—she gulped—"*blue.*"

I climbed off the boat. "I think we might need to have a little chat with Owen," I said.

But when we went inside the lodge, Owen was nowhere to be found. His ladder sat empty against the wall. The paint supplies were gone.

"Where do you suppose he's run off to?" George said.

"And why?" said Bess.

"I don't know," I answered, inspecting the trim Owen had been painting. "One thing I do know. . . . That is definitely the same color paint that was used to vandalize the *Sail Away.*"

Later that evening, we gathered in Megan's kitchen for dinner. Megan was at the butcher-block island, chopping zucchini. George, Bess, and I sat on stools on the opposite side.

"I hope you like zucchini," Megan said. "I signed up for a CSA—that stands for community-supported agriculture. Each week I get a basket of fresh fruits and veggies, and this week was heavy on zucchini. So tonight we're having ham-and-zucchini casserole, zucchini bread, and air-fried zucchini slices."

"Sounds good to me!" George replied.

I filled Megan in on the matching paint colors and asked her about Owen.

"How long has he been working for you?" I said.

"About two months," Megan answered, still chopping. "I hired him shortly after I moved in, to paint and do some minor carpentry work."

"And where did you find him?" I said.

"Funny thing," Megan said, pausing with her knife mid-chop. "I didn't find him as much as he found me."

"What do you mean?" Bess asked.

"Well," Megan said, "he basically turned up one day. Said he'd heard about the resort and club. That he was a handyman and wondered if I had any odd jobs I needed done. His rates were good and he seemed like a decent guy, so I hired him."

"Did you check his Yelp reviews first?" George asked.

"Uh yeah, no—this isn't exactly the sort of place where handymen have Yelp reviews," Megan said with a laugh. "Half the town still uses landlines, not cell phones. You don't think Owen had something to do with this, do you?"

I wasn't sure yet. He had seemed a little . . . twitchy when we met. "Worth checking out," I said. "What did the sheriff have to say?"

Megan set down her knife and shrugged. "Not much. Said he'd file a report, but not to worry. He thinks the whole thing was probably a prank. Bored kids, trying to be funny."

"Wow, I don't see what's so funny about that," Bess said.

"Me either," George said.

"I agree. If it was a prank, it was a pretty terrible one," I said.

"True," Megan said. "But I'd prefer to think the sheriff is right. Beats the alternative, right? I'd rather not think somebody is out to get me or the club. The blue paint came off with some acetone and scrubbing. Unfortunately, it took the original name off with it, but Owen said he can fix that for me. It will be fine. So tell me, are you all settled in? How's your room?"

"Oh, it's perfect," I said. "I love the window seat with the view of the lake! We can't thank you enough for having us."

"The bunk beds are fabulous too," Bess said. "So fun. Reminds me of summer camp!"

"I'm glad you're comfortable," Megan said. "You'll have to come back and spend a few nights at the guest lodge in the fall when the leaves change color. As long as Mr. Plath doesn't come up with some last-minute objection to our opening . . ."

My detective radar pinged again.

"About Mr. Plath," I said, finally getting a chance to ask about something else that had been bothering me all afternoon. "You said he's been a thorn in your side since day one. But what was all that talk about a captain not wanting you here either?"

Megan pulled a stack of plates from a cabinet and set them on the counter, alongside some silverware and napkins. "Would you all mind setting the table while I finish dinner and we can chat then?"

"Of course!" George said, grabbing the plates.

We placed the settings around the kitchen table while Megan layered her zucchini slices in a baking dish with diced ham and a creamy sauce. She slid the pan into the oven and rinsed her hands in the sink. Then she pulled a tray of cheese and crackers from the refrigerator and placed it on the kitchen island.

"Dig in," she said. "Local cheddar. It's the best."

George grabbed a slice and popped it into her mouth. "Delicious!"

Bess and I each took a piece and nodded appreciatively. I swallowed.

"The captain?" I said, nudging the conversation away from cheese and back to Megan's cranky neighbor's odd comment. "Does he or she live nearby too?"

"Right. The infamous Captain Stone," Megan said. "No, he doesn't live nearby. Well, not unless you believe in ghosts. Captain Stone ran a tavern on this property after the Revolutionary War. People around here like to say his ghost still haunts this land."

"So *that's* what our server at the airport was talking about," Bess said. "She said the old resort was haunted. Seemed sort of freaked out by him."

"Yeah, people say that the captain is the reason nobody has been successful developing out here," Megan said. "That's why I got such a good deal on the land. Nobody wanted it. It's cursed or something like that."

I glanced out the window at the serene view. The sun was setting over the distant mountains and sending streaks of orange and gold across the smooth surface of the lake. It was a postcard image, if I ever saw one. It was hard to believe nobody wanted this property, curse or no curse. Maybe nobody wanted to deal with Mr. Plath. . . .

The conversation turned to summer plans, family

news, and other casual chitchat. But my mind kept circling back to the rumors of a curse and ghost. There had to be something behind them, right?

A timer dinged. Megan grabbed a pot holder and pulled her bubbling zucchini casserole from the oven. It smelled incredible!

"Dinner's ready!" she said.

We sat at the kitchen table, filled our plates, and dug in.

"I never knew zucchini could taste so good," Bess said.

"Thanks," Megan said. "But I hope next week I'll get something a *little* different. Like maybe a potato or a couple of onions, at least."

I stuck an air-fried zucchini slice into my mouth and chewed, still thinking about the "curse." I have a serious need for things to add up. If they don't, I really can't concentrate on anything else. And something about this case wasn't adding up. Okay, I knew it wasn't *officially* a case. Or it wasn't my case, at least. It was in the hands of the local sheriff, who as far as I could tell wasn't terribly interested in solving it.

Which, if you asked me, made it my case by default.

"So why do people think Captain Stone haunts this property?" I asked.

Megan shrugged. "People say strange things used to happen at the old resort. Lights flickering. Cold drafts in the hallways. That sort of thing."

"Seems like all that could be pretty easily explained," I said. "It is pretty windy out here, after all."

"Exactly," Megan said. "Of course, there was the suspicious fire that burned the old resort to the ground. I don't think they ever figured out what caused that. Far easier—and much more entertaining—to blame it on the ghost of some long-gone sea captain, right?"

"True," I mumbled, taking another bite. Though if all my years of sleuthing had taught me anything, people didn't go around blaming ghosts. Not unless they were trying to cover up their own misdeeds.

"Anyway, enough of that!" Megan said. "There aren't any ghosts here. I'm sure it will all get sorted out. I've worked too hard to let some silly prank throw me off my game. In the meantime, I really need to do something to thank Ricky for all his help today. I was thinking a nice pie."

"Zucchini pie?" I asked.

"Ha," Megan answered. "No, there's a general store in town that sells beautiful pies. Thought I'd run there in the morning and grab one. Before I finish polishing the boat one last time and getting the menu for the barbecue finalized with the caterer for the grand opening celebration and . . ." She rubbed the back of her neck, looked down at her booted foot, and sighed.

"Hey," I said. "I have a better idea. How about Bess, George, and I run into town in the morning instead? We can pick up a pie. And when we get back, we can help you with the rest of it."

"You wouldn't mind?" Megan said. "I feel bad. This was supposed to be a vacation for you three."

"Of course we wouldn't mind," Bess piped up. "We're happy to help!"

"Also, we love pie," George added with a grin.

And, I thought—but didn't say—a trip into town

would be a great excuse to poke around. See if I could dig up any dirt. I wanted to know more about this Captain Stone guy, the old Gemstone Islands Resort, and what *really* caused that fire.

Because something told me there was a whole lot more to the story.

And a whole lot more than animals and bored kids causing mischief around Megan's property.

CHAPTER FIVE

Digging for Clues

I WOKE UP THE NEXT MORNING TO THE sound of wind chimes clanging in the breeze that wafted through the open bedroom window. After getting dressed for the day in a comfy pair of shorts and a T-shirt, I headed downstairs for breakfast with George and Bess. Megan had left fresh fruit and cereal on the kitchen table, along with her car keys, some money, and a note thanking us for picking up a pie.

As we ate, I watched Megan through the kitchen window. She was hobbling along the dock, checking and rechecking the lines that secured the *Sail Away*.

Then, after she gave the front line one final yank, she knelt and awkwardly scrubbed the boat's hull with a sponge.

"Maybe we should go out there and see if she needs any help," I said.

"Good idea," Bess said.

We cleared our dishes and went outside onto the cottage's back porch. The birds were chirping happily in the trees. Jimmy Chew was curled on the lawn, gnawing on a stick. The sun was out and it looked like a beautiful day ahead.

"Hi, Megan!" I shouted, and waved.

"Good morning!" She waved back. "How was breakfast?"

"Perfect," George answered. "Thank you!"

"We wondered if you needed any help before we went into town," I said.

Megan shook her head. "No, you girls go ahead. Have fun. Maybe explore a little. I have it under control here. Just getting things nice and shiny!"

She walked to the foot of the dock and opened

the storage locker. She scratched her head, frowning.

"What is it?" I asked. "Is something wrong?"

Megan's eyebrows knit together. "You put the life jackets back in here yesterday, right?"

"Yeah, we put them back right away," I said.

"Why?" Bess asked.

"It's just that they're . . . gone." Megan pointed. "All the spare life jackets are gone."

George, Bess, and I joined her on the dock. I peered inside the open locker. The only thing left was a thin layer of mucky water on the bottom. Not a single life jacket. Even in all the commotion yesterday afternoon, I was certain we'd put them away.

"That's weird. Why would someone take your life jackets?" Bess asked.

"I don't know," she said, her frown deepening. "Maybe someone borrowed them and forgot to put them back?"

"Before you woke up this morning?" I said skeptically.

"I'll have to ask Owen if he saw anything," Megan said.

George's gaze drifted past us, toward the lodge's back porch. "Hey, is that a security camera?" she asked. Megan turned around and looked.

"Oh, yeah. It is," Megan said. "I put it in so I could keep an eye on things down here on the dock, especially during bad weather."

"You have video of the dock, then?" I asked excitedly. "That might tell us who has been down here!"

"Unfortunately, I don't," Megan said, shoulders slumping. "I haven't been able to get the system to work properly. As far as I can tell, the camera is recording—the green light is on and everything. But for some reason, I can't access the video footage. And I consider myself pretty tech savvy. But honestly, I've had so much to do around here, the camera fell pretty far to the bottom of my list and I kind of forgot about it. Now I wish I hadn't. . . ."

George squared her shoulders. "No worries," she said. "I can help you with that!"

"Really?" Megan said.

"It's true," I said. "I've never met anyone as good

with technology as George. If there's any way to recover that video, George will figure out how."

"That would be amazing!" Megan said.

"Great," George answered. "What sort of network are you set up on?"

While George and Megan discussed the ins and outs of WANs and LANs, I tapped Bess on the shoulder. "Maybe we should run to the store for the pie while they figure out the camera system?"

"That would be great," Megan cut in. "Do you mind staying back here, George?"

"Not at all," she said. "As long as Nancy and Bess remember to get some pie for me, too!"

"Ha, no problem," I answered.

Bess and I went back inside and grabbed the car keys. As we drove away from the cottage, I rolled down the window and listened. The tires crunched loudly over the loose gravel.

"You hear that?" I asked. Bess nodded.

"Yeah, why?" she said.

"Loud, huh?"

Bess nodded. "So?"

"I'm just thinking," I said. "If someone came down here last night by car and stole those life jackets, we would have heard them drive in, right? The windows were open."

"Unless we were asleep," Bess said.

"Maybe," I said. "Though George's snoring kept waking me up. I think I would have heard a car, too."

"You think the thief was on foot?" Bess said.

"Seems that way," I answered. Which narrowed down our suspect list dramatically. Unless, of course, the culprit had parked at the top of the driveway and walked down. That seemed quite risky, though. Not to mention, there was nowhere to discreetly park a car on this narrow road.

I continued mulling over the possibilities as we drove alongside the field of swaying wildflowers. Something caught my eye. I tapped the brakes and did a double take. Bess bounced forward in her seat.

"Sorry," I said. "But is that Mr. Plath?" I pointed at a white-haired man standing in the field. He was leaning heavily on something. His cane?

Bess craned her neck for a better view. "Sure looks like it. What on earth is he doing out there in the middle of the field?"

Just then Mr. Plath raised his arms above his head, and something shiny and silver glinted in the sun. Not his cane. A *shovel*. He swung it back down, connecting with earth, and flung it upward again. Clumps of dirt and plant roots flew around.

"It looks like he's . . . *digging*?" I answered.

"Digging? Why would he be digging out there?" Bess said.

"That is a very good question. . . ."

A small beep jolted me from my thoughts. I glanced in the rearview mirror to see a car approaching. I waved and mouthed, *Sorry*, then stepped on the accelerator. But my mind was back in the field with Mr. Plath. Why *was* he digging out there?

"Maybe he was picking flowers?" Bess said.

"With a shovel, though?" I answered. "Who picks flowers with a shovel? And why go all the way to the middle of the field if you only wanted a few flowers? Also, Mr. Plath doesn't really strike me as the type to collect bouquets. Unless they're made of poison ivy . . ."

"Ha-ha," Bess said with a laugh. "But you're right. It's weird."

It was. In fact, there were an awful lot of weird things going on. I suddenly thought of the hole Megan had stepped in yesterday, twisting her foot. Did Mr. Plath have something to do with that, too? And could it be connected with the vandalism on the dock?

I had a lot of questions.

We arrived in the village of Burnham. I parked in front of the Gemstone Islands General Store, aka GIGS, according to the hand-painted wooden sign out front. The store was tucked into the first floor of a quaint, blue-painted Victorian house with gingerbread trim. Bess and I walked up the white front steps and across the porch. A pair of weathered rocking chairs flanked the entrance. When we pushed the door open, a little bell jingled, announcing our arrival.

"Look," Bess squealed. "They have handmade

jewelry!" She hurried to a display of necklaces, bracelets, and earrings opposite the register. "What do you think?" she said, holding up a pair of hammered metal earrings painted sky blue.

"Adorable," I said.

"Ah, I already have too much jewelry," Bess said with a sigh. She returned the earrings to the display.

We explored the narrow aisles, the well-worn hardwood floors creaking with every step we took. The store's shelves were jam-packed with a little bit of everything: fishing lures, canned soup, bread, bulk candy, jugs of syrup, foam water floats, and more.

I picked up a small toy bone. "Do you think Jimmy Chew would like this?"

"Absolutely!" Bess said. She grabbed a box of pure maple candy shaped like miniature maple leaves. "And I'd like this! You can't have too much maple, right?"

"Agreed," I answered. We browsed a bit more, picking up some salted caramel chocolates for George. I selected a green "Champ" lake monster key chain for my boyfriend, Ned. Bess and I could probably spend half a day in here browsing, but we had work to do.

And a case to solve . . .

"Okay, so where do you think they keep the pies?" I asked Bess.

"Hopefully not in there." Bess pointed at a glass-doored refrigerator that was labeled LIVE BAIT and stacked with containers of worms.

I laughed.

We found the baked items at the rear of the store, artfully displayed in a large plexiglass case. There were cookies, muffins, doughnuts, and yes—pies. All sorts of pies. Cherry, chocolate cream, strawberry rhubarb, and apple. My mouth watered.

An older woman with short, curly gray hair and a name tag that read WINNIE shuffled behind the case and smiled. "Hello!" she said brightly. "What can I get for you today?"

"That is a good question," I said. "Everything looks delicious! We need a pie or two. What do you recommend?"

"They're all quite good," Winnie answered. "Can't

go wrong with apple, of course. And the strawberry rhubarb is always a crowd-pleaser. Myself, I like the cherry."

"What do you think, Bess?" I said.

"I think the chocolate cream looks amazing," she answered.

"Well, that doesn't help narrow it down!" I laughed. Winnie grinned. "You know," I said. "Since we can't decide, I think we'll just take one of each. How's that?"

"Now you're talking," Bess said. "You're going to be George's hero!"

Winnie pulled four white pie boxes from beneath the case. As she assembled them, I seized the opportunity to ask her a few questions.

"This is a beautiful town," I said. "Have you lived here long?"

"Ah-yup," Winnie answered, sliding a whipped-cream-covered chocolate pie into a box. I could practically taste the shaved chocolate sprinkled on top. Winnie closed the lid and sealed the box shut with a piece of shiny tape. She reached for the next pie.

"It's our first time here," I continued. "My friend Megan bought the old Gemstone Islands Resort property."

Winnie glanced up, then went back to packing pies. "You don't say?"

"You must remember the old resort, then?" I asked.

"Ah-yup," Winnie answered.

"Heard it was quite the place, back in the day," I said.

The only thing that got out of Winnie was another "Ah-yup." I glanced at Bess and shrugged.

"We also heard it's haunted by some old sea captain," Bess said. "I'd *love* to hear that story!"

Winnie didn't say anything to that. Not even an *ah-yup*.

"I'd like to hear that story too," I said.

"Nothing to hear," Winnie said. She stacked our filled pie boxes, pasted a smile on her face, and handed them to me. "Will that be all?"

"I think so," I answered, a bit deflated. Were all the locals this talkative . . . ?

"Okay," Winnie said. "Come around front and I'll ring you up, then."

We followed the *swish-swish* of Winnie's long green dress as she walked toward the front of the store, passing a teenage girl who was restocking the chip aisle. The girl stopped, holding a bag of cheese curls midair, and watched us go by with a quizzical look on her face.

We reached the register and placed our items on the wooden counter. Unlike most stores, GIGS didn't have any price scanners. Instead Winnie read the bright orange tag attached to each item and entered the prices into the register, one by one. The silence hung heavily in the air while she worked. I wanted to ask more questions, but Winnie didn't look up.

"That'll be forty-two dollars and fifty-five cents," she said when she was done punching buttons.

I handed her the money. She stacked our pies and goodies into a brown paper bag and slid it across the counter.

"You all have a good day and enjoy your visit," she

said with a smile. "Thanks for shopping at GIGS. Come back again soon!"

"Thanks," I answered. "You have a nice day too."

Bess and I headed back outside and down the steps into the gravel parking lot.

"Well, that didn't amount to much," I said, slightly frustrated.

"But we did get some delicious pies," Bess said, licking her lips.

"There is that!" I opened the car's trunk and placed the bag inside.

The door jangled at the top of the stairs. I glanced up to see the teenage shelf-stocker jogging our way. She was younger than I'd thought when we first walked by—maybe thirteen or fourteen at the most—with big brown eyes and dark hair pulled into a high ponytail. She waved at us.

"Hey!" she said. "Hold on a minute."

I closed the trunk. The girl ran up.

"Hi," she said. Her name tag read MELINA.

"Hi," I answered. "Is everything okay? Did we drop

something in there?" I checked my pockets. Phone, money, and car keys were all there.

"No," Melina said. "It's just . . . I heard you asking about the Gemstone Islands Resort. And *Captain Stone*," she added in a whisper, eyes darting around.

Bess walked to the back of the car and stood next to us, eyebrows raised.

"Yes," I said. "We were curious. Sounded like an interesting legend. I love to learn about the history of places I visit."

"Oh, he's no legend," Melina said breathlessly. "He's *real*." She glanced over her shoulder and back at the store, as if an apparition might suddenly appear at the top of the stairs and jump out at her.

"He is?" I asked.

"Oh yeah, he most definitely is," she said. "I would know! I've seen him with my own eyes."

CHAPTER SIX

The Ghost of Captain Stone

WELL, MELINA DEFINITELY HAD MY attention now.

"What?" I asked. "You've seen Captain Stone?"

She nodded vigorously. "Sure have. I live upstairs. This is my parents' store. Which is how I get stuck working here every summer." She rolled her eyes and jutted her thumb over her shoulder. "Anyway, been hearing the ghost stories about Captain Stone my whole life. He's supposedly been haunting the Gemstone Islands peninsula forever. I never really believed it. Always thought it was just a bunch of talk. Until last month."

"Really? What happened last month?" I asked, intrigued.

"I was camping with my Girl Scout troop a few weeks ago," Melina said. "We go on a camping trip every year. This year, our troop leader got permission for us to camp up at Pirate's Perch. You know it?"

"We've heard about it," Bess said.

"Yeah, right, okay," Melina continued. "So everyone was kind of spooked to camp up there. Got even worse at night. Everyone was telling ghost stories and stuff and trying to freak each other out. I was sharing a tent with my friends Emma and Lanie and I couldn't fall asleep. Not because of the ghost stories, but because Emma was snoring so loud. It's the worst! She doesn't believe she does it either. But one of these days I'm going to take my phone and record her!" Melina huffed. I could sympathize—after all, George's snores sound like someone sawing through a tin can with a knife. But I wanted Melina to get back on track. I gave her an encouraging nod.

"And . . . ?" I said.

"Right," she said. "I couldn't sleep, so I climbed out of the tent. We're not really supposed to leave the campsite, but I wasn't going far. Just thought I'd look around a little and see if I could spot anything cool. Like a deer or fox or something."

"Did you?" Bess asked.

"No," Melina said. "But I did hear this funny scraping sound coming from near the trail. It was really foggy that night and hard to see through the trees. I crept toward the sound so whatever it was wouldn't hear me coming. And that's when I saw him. Captain Stone!"

"Whoa," Bess said.

"How did you know it was Captain Stone?" I asked.

"Well, he was wearing a long coat and one of those funny three-cornered hats like a pirate, so who else would it be?" she said with a shrug.

I didn't point out that just about anyone could be dressed in a topcoat and hat. What mattered at the moment was what Melina *thought* she saw.

"And get this . . . ," she continued, leaning forward with her eyebrows raised.

"Yes?" I said.

"The captain was digging in the dirt with a big shovel!"

Melina stopped talking briefly as a man and woman walked past us and into the store. The bell jingled, then went quiet again.

"He was digging?" I asked, the little hairs on my neck pricking up.

"Yeah. So I ran back to the tent to grab my phone so I could take a picture," Melina said. "My pajamas didn't have pockets, you know, and my phone was back in my sleeping bag. But I guess Captain Stone must have heard me. Because when I got back, he was gone."

"Oh," I said, feeling my shoulders sag a little.

"There's more, though!" Melina said. "He left me a message." She scrabbled in her pocket and pulled out a phone. She tapped the screen and swung it in my direction.

My eyes widened as I read the message "Captain Stone" had left written in the dirt. A very familiar message:

Stay away.

This could not be a coincidence.

"Did you tell anyone what you saw?" I asked Melina.

"Everyone," Melina said with an eye roll. "But nobody believed me! Thought I was playing a prank. Or trying to get attention. I guess it's okay for a bunch of old people to have Captain Stone ghost stories from a hundred years ago about how he made them lose a big fish or turned the weather bad. But when I—"

The door to GIGS jangled again. Winnie stepped out and stood at the top of the stairs, hands on her hips.

"Melina," she said. "What are you doing out here? We have customers."

"Sorry, Grandma!" Melina said.

Winnie glanced between me, Bess, and Melina. She squinted. "You were listening to us back in the store, weren't you?"

Melina didn't answer.

Winnie sighed. "And let me guess, you came out

here to tell these nice young ladies about the time you 'saw' Captain Stone up at the perch."

Melina shrugged.

"All right, you," Winnie said with a shake of her head. "You run back inside and quit scaring the flat-landers with your ghost stories. We have some customers who need sandwiches made."

"Okay," Melina said, and waved to us. "Bye! Nice to meet you. And be careful out there! I don't know what Captain Stone wants. But I don't think he was happy to see me!" She dodged back up the stairs, past Winnie—who was still shaking her head—and into the store.

"Sorry about that," Winnie said. "Melina's a great girl. But she's also got a great big imagination."

"It's all good," I said. "We enjoyed talking to her."

"Ah-yup," Winnie answered, then went back into the store without another word. Bess and I got into the car. I pushed the ignition and sat there a moment, thinking.

"That was . . . interesting," I finally said, and put

the car in reverse. We pulled onto the main road and began the drive back to Megan's resort.

"Interesting?" Bess said. "More like creepy! Do you think there's really a ghost out there?"

"A ghost?" I said. "No. But I don't think Melina was playing a prank, either."

"So you think she saw someone?" Bess said.

I nodded. "The question is who? And why?"

"And why do they want everyone to 'stay away'?" Bess said.

❦

CHAPTER SEVEN

Muddy Shovels

BESS AND I CARRIED THE PIES AND presents back into Megan's house. Jimmy Chew went completely bananas when I gave him the bone. George was nearly as excited when she got her chocolate. If she had a tail, I'm pretty sure it would have been wagging too. At least she didn't flop on her back begging for belly rubs.

"Any luck with the security video?" I asked.

George shook her head. "Tried everything I could think of but couldn't get it to work."

"Oh. How's the foot?" I nodded at Megan, who

was sitting at the kitchen table with her boot propped on an adjoining chair.

"Keeping it elevated," she answered. "I'm sure I've already violated the doctor's advice to stay off it a thousand times over." She sighed. "Thanks so much for running to GIGS and getting the pies. And Jimmy's treat!"

Jimmy woofed.

"Happy to do it." I contemplated the boot on Megan's foot. I thought about Melina's story. I pictured Mr. Plath out digging in the field. "Where did you say you stepped in that hole again? I'd like to check it out."

"Up at Pirate's Perch," Megan said.

Bess and I exchanged a knowing look. "Interesting . . . ," we said at the same time.

"Hey, what's that all about?" George asked.

"Long story," I said. "I'll explain while we walk. Could you point us in the direction of Pirate's Perch, Megan?"

"Sure," she answered. "The trail starts around the corner, right past Charlotte's house. Do you still have the map you picked up yesterday at the lodge? It will show you how to get there."

"Yes, it's in our room," I said. "I'll grab it."

I ran upstairs and got the map.

"Oh, and Nancy?" Megan said when I returned. "Would you girls mind dropping one of those pies off to Ricky and Charlotte on your way to the perch? You can't miss their place. It's the only house between here and the trails."

"Sure, no problem!" I said, grabbing the strawberry rhubarb pie.

As George, Bess, and I headed toward Charlotte's, I filled George in on Melina's story.

"Very strange," George said. "Obviously not a ghost, but still strange."

"I agree," I said. "There's very clearly something else going on around here."

"What do you think it is?" Bess asked.

"That's what I'd like to find out," I said.

We rounded a corner. Off to the right, a driveway led to a tidy wood-framed house perched on a knoll overlooking the lake. It looked like a storybook cottage, with a peaked roofline and second-story dormered windows decorated with flower boxes. "That must be Ricky and Charlotte's place," I said, pointing.

The three of us turned down the stone walkway to the yellow front door. I knocked and waited. After a few moments, the door swung open. A woman with curly white hair and a friendly face sat in a wheelchair on the other side.

"Well, hello!" she said brightly. "You must be friends of Ricky's?"

"Actually, we're friends of Megan's. She asked us to deliver this." I held out the pie. "To thank Ricky for all his help yesterday. You must be Charlotte?"

"Oh, isn't that wonderful! Yes, I'm Charlotte," she said, spinning her wheelchair around and beckoning us inside. "Do come in!"

We slipped off our shoes and followed Charlotte into the main living area. A wall of windows faced the lake, offering a view clear across the water to the Adirondack Mountains. I set the pie on the counter that separated the kitchen from the living room. Charlotte opened the box, inhaled deeply, and smiled.

"Strawberry rhubarb, my favorite!" she exclaimed. "Would you care to join me for a slice?"

"A slice of pie?" George said. "Absolutely!"

I wasn't quite as hungry as George (not sure that's even possible). But pie did sound good. Plus, chatting over a slice would be a good way to ask Charlotte a few questions. Maybe she'd be a little more talkative than Winnie back at GIGS.

"That does sound lovely," I said. "Thank you!"

We sat at the kitchen table. As Charlotte plated the pie, I took note of the shiny gold-and-diamond wedding band on her left hand. Clearly, she was married. However, judging by the two pairs of shoes at the front door—high-top Converse and women's sneakers—Charlotte and Ricky seemed to be the only people who lived there.

"It's so nice to have a full table again," Charlotte said as we dug into our slices. "Can get awfully quiet around here. There was a time when this kitchen would be filled with kids and friends, all trooping through with their wet bathing suits and dripping hair and damp towels." A sad smile crossed her face. "At least I have Ricky to keep me company for now."

"Is it just the two of you?" Bess asked.

Charlotte nodded. "My husband, Arthur, passed a few months back."

"Oh, I'm sorry," George said. Bess and I nodded sympathetically.

"I try to count my blessings," Charlotte said, eyes drifting toward the expansive view out the window with a touch of longing. "Grief is the flip side of love, you know. I was fortunate to have the years I did with my family and a home filled with memories. Arthur actually designed this house, and I still feel his presence in every room and vista. I hear the laughter of my children around this table every time I sit here."

"That's really beautiful," Bess said, blotting the corner of her eye with a napkin.

"Thank you," Charlotte said. "And thanks for the pie. It's simply delicious!"

"You're welcome," I answered. "Can't take credit for the pie, though. It was Megan's idea. We just picked it up from GIGS."

"Oh, so you've been to GIGS," Charlotte said, eyes brightening. "Quite the quirky little store, isn't it? What did you think?"

"It was adorable!" Bess said. "I could have spent hours in there."

George nodded, chewing at the same time. "It's true," she said. "Bess could spend hours shopping just about anywhere. Department stores, high-end boutiques, roadside truck stops . . ."

Bess gave her cousin a friendly little slug on the arm.

I cleared my throat. This seemed like a good opportunity to ask Charlotte a few questions about Melina's stories. "We met a nice young clerk there," I said, spearing a piece of pie and twirling it in the air. "Melina? Told us she camped out with her Girl Scout troop here on your property a few weeks ago."

"Oh yes, that's right," Charlotte said. "Melina.

Sweet kid. Kind of has a crush on Ricky, I think. . . ." Charlotte glanced around. "Where has that boy wandered off to, anyway? He's impossible to keep track of . . . loves these woods and trails and lake more than anything. Think he'd live out there, if that was an option." She took a bite of pie. "Anyway, I'm rambling! You were saying something about Melina?"

"Yes!" Bess cut in. "She told us she saw a ghost. At Pirate's Perch!"

"A ghost?" Charlotte said, eyebrows raised.

"That's right. She told us she saw the ghost of Captain Stone," I said. "And that he was up at Pirate's Perch digging a hole."

"Ahhh," Charlotte said with a shake of her head. "Good old Captain Stone. Let me guess, he was up there digging for buried treasure?"

"Buried treasure?" Bess, George, and I said in unison.

"Oh, so she didn't tell you the rest, then?" Charlotte said. "I'm surprised."

"She didn't get a chance. Her grandmother called her back into the store," I said.

"Oh yes, Winnie runs a tight ship," Charlotte said. "That store's been in the family for generations. They can't afford to let things slide, not with the big supermarket that just opened down the way in Colchester."

Interesting. Maybe that explained why Winnie didn't want her granddaughter "scaring away" the tourists with "ghost stories."

"What's the rest of the story, then?" George said.

"Right. Folks around here seem to think Captain Stone buried a bunch of treasure somewhere on the peninsula," Charlotte said. "Used to get all sorts of treasure hunters poking around. It's why we posted the property with 'No Trespassing' signs many years back. Seemed to put a stop to it. At least I thought so."

My friends and I exchanged looks.

"Do you think someone might be back searching again?" I asked, leaning forward.

Charlotte shrugged. "I guess it's possible, though it doesn't seem very likely. Truthfully, my husband Arthur was the worst of them all. The stories he used to tell our kids, oh my! He and our Judy used to spend hours studying maps and roaming the peninsula with metal detectors. They were sure they'd find that treasure," she said with a sad smile.

"But they didn't?" Bess said.

"Of course not. Seems to me if there was a hidden treasure, someone would have unearthed it by now, don't you think? Captain Stone has been little more than a memory—and a fanciful story—for two hundred-plus years. That ship, as they say, sailed a long time ago." Charlotte held up her pie server. "Now, who'd like another slice?"

George raised her hand. "Me, please. Thank you!"

Charlotte scooped a generous piece of pie onto George's plate.

I glanced around the living area. The wood-paneled walls were decorated with dozens of family photos. Charlotte and a man with twinkling eyes like Ricky's—Arthur, I assumed—through the years as they held babies, traveled, sat by the lake. I made out several of a clearly younger Ricky holding up a fresh-caught fish, riding a bike, climbing a tree. There were other pictures of two young girls, probably five years apart in age. One girl had curly red hair. The other was blond, like Ricky. Judging from their clothing, I'd guess the pictures had been taken more than thirty years ago. There were more recent photos of the blond-haired girl, now a woman, but none of the redhead.

My eyes roamed next to a large, ornately framed portrait of a young woman. She looked like a younger version of Charlotte, with the same blue eyes and curly hair. But the dress and formal hairstyle of the woman in the portrait seemed way too old-fashioned to be Charlotte. I pointed at it with my fork.

"That's a beautiful painting," I said.

Bess glanced over to see what I was gesturing at. "Oh, it sure is! Is that you, Charlotte?"

Charlotte laughed. "Me? Heavens no. I'm old, but I'm not that old! That's my great-great-great—I'm not exactly sure how many greats, to be honest—grandmother, Elizabeth."

"She's beautiful," I said. "I can definitely see the resemblance."

Charlotte smiled. "Thank you. Getting harder and harder to see it through all these wrinkles. Getting harder to see, period." She chuckled. I liked Charlotte. She was sweet and funny, even though a small cloud of sadness and loss seemed to hover around her.

We ate our pie and chatted a bit longer. But whenever I tried to steer the conversation back toward Captain Stone or the treasure, Charlotte deftly steered it to something else. I decided not to press. For whatever reason, all that treasure talk was clearly a touchy subject. Maybe because she'd lost her husband so recently and it had been an obsession of his.

When the last crumbs of pie had been devoured from our plates, Bess, George, and I cleared our dishes and thanked Charlotte.

"This has been really nice," I said. "You have a beautiful home."

"Yes, thank you!" Bess and George agreed.

"You're very welcome," Charlotte said. "It's been lovely having you. Please, come back and visit anytime."

As we made our way toward the front door, another picture caught my eye: an image of a large white-painted building on the lake. The three Gemstone Islands were visible in the background. A young couple holding a baby stood in front of the building, smiling, next to a sign that read GEMSTONE ISLANDS RESORT.

That must be the old resort people had been talking about. It was beautiful. Megan wasn't kidding when she said she'd scaled back her design. The original Gemstone Islands Resort stood probably five stories high and incorporated a replica lighthouse on one side and a wraparound porch on the other.

"Arthur designed that, too," Charlotte said when she saw where I was looking. "With the exception of this house, he was most proud of that building. There was a three-hundred-and-sixty-degree view from the top of the lighthouse." Another sad smile crossed her face.

I was about to ask her more when the front door swung open. Ricky came barreling through and skidded to a stop. He reminded me, and not in a minor way, of Jimmy Chew. Particularly when he'd just come inside from hiding a bone.

"Oh!" Ricky said, jolting back in surprise at the sight of us in the foyer. His blond hair flopped over his eyes and he swiped it away. "I'm sorry. I didn't expect to see you here."

"Sorry to surprise you," I said. "We're on our way to Pirate's Perch. Stopped by to drop off a pie for you and your grandmother. Megan wanted to thank you for your help yesterday."

"Oh, it was no problem!" Ricky said, smiling. "Glad I was in the right place at the right time." He took a step forward.

Charlotte glanced at his boots. They were caked with mud, as were his hands and clothes. There was even some dirt smudged across his right cheek. "Ricky," she said with an exasperated sigh. "How many times do I have to tell you not to wear those muddy things in here?"

"Sorry, Nana," he said with a sheepish grin. He slipped off the boots and stuck them by the welcome mat.

"What have you been up to anyway?" Charlotte said. "You're a mess!"

"Nothing," Ricky said, shrugging. "Just, um . . . out for a walk." He glanced past us and chewed his bottom lip.

A walk? I wasn't sure what kind of walk could get a person so dirty. It looked more like Ricky had been out rolling in mud puddles. *Odd* . . .

"Well," I said, "we don't want to keep you any longer. Thanks for sharing the pie!"

"You saved me a piece, right?" Ricky asked.

"Of course I did," Charlotte said. "Just get yourself cleaned up first and I'll plate you a slice. And thanks for coming by, girls!" She gave us a wave.

We said goodbye and headed outside. When we reached the end of Charlotte's walkway, I looked back over my shoulder at her house. *Interesting* . . .

A shovel was now propped against the wood siding, out of view of the front door. Clumps of dirt clung to the bottom—just like they had to Ricky's hands, clothes, and boots.

CHAPTER EIGHT

Pirate's Perch

NOW, THERE'S NOTHING PARTICULARLY suspicious about a shovel. Many people have shovels. We have one in our shed at home. Hannah, my dad's housekeeper, and I used it to plant a vegetable garden in our backyard last summer.

But.

A shovel, plus "Captain Stone" sightings, plus rumors of a mysterious buried treasure?

Well, in my book, that's a clue.

A whole bunch of them, in fact.

"Do you see that?" I asked Bess and George.

"See what?" Bess asked.

"That shovel leaning against the side of Charlotte's house," I said. "It wasn't there when we arrived."

"Interesting," George said. "Ricky was awfully muddy when he came inside too."

"Exactly. Like perhaps he'd been digging?" I said.

"Do you think there's any truth to what Charlotte was saying?" Bess said. "About a buried treasure?" Her voice notched up with excitement. I could tell what she was thinking: Forget shopping. Buried treasure would be the ultimate jewelry haul.

"That's what we're going to find out," I answered.

We began the climb toward Pirate's Perch. The trail grew narrower and steeper the farther we went, and I had to catch my breath more than once. This hike was more challenging than I'd expected.

Bess groaned. "How much farther?" she said. "You know I don't like to hike."

"I'll admit I'm with Bess on this one," George said, huffing. "I'd rather be in the lodge." She swatted her arm and made a face. "The bugs out here are the size of small birds!"

"It can't be much farther," I said. The hill hadn't looked nearly this big from the bottom. Of course, that was the thing about mountains. Like mysteries, you couldn't really tell how far they went until you were climbing them.

All around us, the woods grew thick and dense. A few less-traveled paths extended off the main trail, disappearing into the trees. Bright yellow signs reading NO TRESPASSING: ACCESS BY PERMISSION ONLY were posted alongside them. I paused.

"Where do you think those trails go?" I said, peering down one. I could just make out what looked like a small cabin nestled in the distant trees. It called to me, like a porch light calls to a moth.

"Nancy," George said. "The sign says no trespassing. . . ."

I pulled the trail map from my pocket and unfolded it. "Don't worry. It isn't trespassing, see?" I tapped the map. "Remember, Megan said she had an agreement with Charlotte to hike up here? We have permission. C'mon. I just want to have a little look around."

"Of course you do." Bess groaned again. "My poor feet!"

We walked down the secondary path, twigs and leaves crunching as we went. The air felt cooler and damper the farther we ventured into the forest. I shivered a little. A bird squawked overhead and something rustled in the trees.

"Can we go back to the main path now?" Bess said. "It's kind of creepy back here."

"It's not creepy," I said. "It's nature. I just want to check out this cabin."

We reached the small wood structure. I peeked inside one of the low-hung windows. The one-room cabin was empty, except for what looked like a couple of energy bar wrappers on the floor. There were no lights or plumbing fixtures. It was just a shack. But what was it doing here in the middle of the woods?

"See anything?" George asked.

"Nothing in there," I said with a shrug.

A noise echoed from somewhere deeper in the forest. It sounded like a twig snapping. Leaves rustling. Bess stiffened.

"What was that?" she said. "Do you think there are bears out here? Or coyotes? Can we *please* go back to the main trail now?"

"Yeah," I said. "Okay. Let's go." I'd seen enough. For now. Besides, there could actually be bears or coyotes in these woods. And it was probably best not to stick around and find out.

We hiked back to the main trail. The final climb to the perch was steep. Large rocks and scraggly trees surrounded us on both sides. Then suddenly the vista opened and we were standing on a grass-covered knoll high above the lake. The panoramic view stretched across the glittering water to the mountain range on the other side. It was timeless and breathtaking. I could almost picture an old ship, Captain Stone at the helm, sailing over the glassy surface below.

George pulled out her phone and started snapping pictures.

"This is incredible!" Bess said. "I take back my complaints. This hike was totally worth it."

"Agreed," I said. I allowed myself a moment to enjoy the scenery. The way the water rippled on the lake below. The sunlight that dappled through the trees. I took a deep breath.

Then I got down to business. The hole Megan had stepped in yesterday morning had to be around here somewhere.

The only problem was, I couldn't find one.

I searched the path all around Pirate's Perch, stumped.

"Do you see a hole anywhere?" I asked Bess and George, pacing.

They both shook their heads.

"Maybe it was farther down the path and we missed it?" George said.

"Maybe," I answered. "But I'm sure Megan said she was at the perch when she stepped in it. She was walking Jimmy Chew. . . ."

Aha! That was it. I needed to think like Jimmy.

Where would Jimmy lead Megan?

"Over by the trees," I said.

"Huh?" Bess said. "What about the trees?"

"Sorry," I answered. "Thinking out loud. Megan stepped in the hole while she was walking Jimmy. So she probably walked off the path because he was sniffing out a place to do his business. Dogs, you know."

A cluster of pine trees sat about ten feet off the path. That looked like the perfect doggie potty stop. I walked over and inspected the ground. *Bingo!* A small patch of freshly disturbed earth sat right in front of the trees. I knelt and brushed away a few leaves and pine needles that had fallen on top. Right below, the soil had very clearly been dug up—and then filled back in.

And that wasn't all.

I stood and wiped off my hands. Not even two feet away, there was another patch of overturned earth. It was exactly the same size as the last one. Two more feet from that, there was another recently dug hole that had been covered back up.

"Interesting," I said. Bess and George stood next to me and surveyed the ground.

"What are you thinking, Nancy?" George said.

"Well, I may not be a wildlife expert," I answered. "But I don't know of any animal who would dig a hole—then fill it back in. Only a person would do that. A person who is trying to cover up what they're doing . . ."

CHAPTER NINE

~❧~

Rough Seas Ahead

AS WE HIKED BACK DOWN THE TRAIL, I couldn't stop thinking about what we'd just found. Was someone actually out here digging for treasure? And what was the connection to the vandalism at Megan's? Or was it nothing more than a coincidence?

Could there really be a treasure hidden somewhere out here?

Maybe there was more to the Gemstone Islands name than those three islands. . . .

When we got back to the resort, Megan was on the dock, standing next to the *Sail Away*. She waved us down, a huge smile on her face. It wasn't quite noon, and the sun shone high in the cloudless sky. A gentle breeze blew across the lake.

"Nancy, George, Bess!" Megan said as we joined her. "How was your hike?"

"It was breathtaking," Bess said. George and I both agreed.

"See anything interesting?" Megan asked. "There's an incredible variety of birds in those woods. I even saw an eagle once!"

"We didn't see any eagles," I said. "But I did spot something kind of interesting . . . a cabin, tucked in the trees. What was that doing there?"

"Oh, you must have stumbled on one of the old hunting cabins," Megan said. "You did take quite the hike, then."

"Don't my feet know it!" Bess said with a grimace.

George's face was serious. "People hunt out there?" she asked. "Is it safe to hike those trails?"

"Absolutely," Megan said. "People don't hunt in these woods anymore. It's not allowed. Every now and then the old cabins do attract random campers, though. Unfortunately, they don't always clean up after themselves, which I hate! Empty water bottles, food containers. Just a couple of weeks ago, I found a pile of dirty clothes!"

"Could they have been Ricky's?" I asked, thinking of how Charlotte said he hung out in the woods a lot—and how she didn't want him tracking mud into the house.

"Not unless he's started wearing yoga pants and hot-pink T-shirts that are at least three sizes too small. Too small for me, even. I threw them in the wash and dropped them in the donation bin downtown," Megan said. "You know how I feel about litter and wasting perfectly good items."

"I do," I said, remembering our visits to Megan in the city. Whenever she encountered a piece of trash, she had to pick it up and recycle it properly. Admirable, even though that meant it usually took forever to get anywhere. "You know, I'm curious about something else, too."

"What's that?" Megan asked.

"That hole you stepped in yesterday when you were walking Jimmy? I think we found it. It looked like somebody went up there and filled it back in."

Megan's eyebrows furrowed. "Hmm," she said. "I suppose *that* could have been Ricky. He seemed pretty upset that I'd tripped and fallen. He might have gone back and covered it up so nobody else would trip in it."

Certainly that could explain what Ricky was doing with a shovel today. However, it didn't explain all the other holes. Unless . . .

"His grandmother told us people think there's a treasure buried somewhere out here," Bess said excitedly.

"Oh, I don't know," Megan said. "Sounds like more tall tales to me. The locals love a good yarn, the bigger and more outlandish the better. Anyway, you're supposed to be having some fun. So, how about taking a break from all the sleuthing and taking the *Sail Away* out for a spin? The weather couldn't be more perfect! You know how to sail, right, Nancy?"

"Took lessons every summer," I said. "And I just went sailing with Ned and his family last weekend too, so I got some good practice in. Plus, there's always a motor if I forget," I added jokingly. "You sure you don't mind?"

"I insist!" Megan said. "You came here to have a good time, right? So have one! I even packed a picnic lunch. It's already on board, along with life jackets for each of you."

"You found the missing life jackets?" Bess asked.

"No, I have others," Megan said. "But I did put a lock on the storage bin. Hate that I have to do it, but I guess it's necessary. Now, what are you waiting for? I have a lot to do around here. Don't need you three in my way." She winked. "So go!"

My friends and I zipped inside to change into our bathing suits and grab towels. I took a big gulp of warm air as we crossed the lawn to the dock. Megan was right—the weather was perfect. Sunny, but not too hot. Windy, but not too windy. A great day to sail!

We reached the dock. Megan held the boat steady

while Bess, George, and I climbed aboard. The *Sail Away* had a typical build, with a ladder leading down to a small center cabin, a deck along the front, a row of seats, and steering at the back—aka aft—of the boat. We dropped our things inside the cabin, which had a small kitchen and two narrow beds, and headed back outside. We pulled on our life jackets and tightened the straps.

"Ready?" Megan asked.

I nodded.

"Great!" she said. "Also, you shouldn't need them, but the emergency kit and radio are in the cabinet next to the sink. All brand-new and good to go. Set them all up yesterday. Now, let's get you on the water. The wind is blowing west, so you don't even need the motor to cast off the dock."

"You mean we can sail away on the *Sail Away*?" George said, and then cracked up.

Bess groaned. "That was a dad joke if I ever heard one." We all laughed at that.

We raised the sails. Megan untied the boat and

gave a push to cast us off while I steered. We cleared the cove easily, and the gentle wind carried us across the smooth surface of the lake. I sucked in a deep breath of the fresh air and tilted my face toward the warm sun. It was so exhilarating to sail again!

We navigated around the lake, tacking back and forth in a zigzag pattern while we snacked on our picnic lunch and admired the scenery. Trees, beaches, and small cottages dotted the shoreline. We passed an osprey sitting atop a tall nest, watching us from its perch. It took flight as we drifted by.

"Now *this* is a vacation," Bess said, stretching out in the sunshine. "I could do this all day!"

"Absolutely!" George agreed. She popped a fresh strawberry into her mouth and smiled.

Time flew. Before I knew it, we had been sailing for nearly two hours.

Unfortunately, that wasn't all that changed.

Without warning, the wind shifted and began to pick up from the west. Dark clouds gathered in the distance over the peaks of the Adirondack Mountains.

It was just after two p.m., yet the darkening sky made it feel much later. A hint of cool air grazed the back of my neck—the telltale sign of an impending storm.

"I think we'd better head in," I said. "Looks like we have some weather headed our way."

"Wow, you're right," Bess said, rubbing the goose bumps that had sprouted on her arms. "That sure came on quick. It got really cold, really fast."

"Let's get moving," I said, gripping the tiller. "Ready about!"

"Ready!" George and Bess responded.

"Lee ho!" I shouted. The boom swung overhead and we ducked. I held tight to the tiller as the *Sail Away* turned in the direction of the resort. As we tacked back and forth, sails fluttering and then snapping tight, my arms began to tire. The wind picked up. The chop on the lake increased and waves lapped against the hull.

Small raindrops began to fall.

I picked out Pirate's Perch, looming high on the hill above. That meant technically the club wasn't far—just around the corner on the other side of the cove. Maybe ten minutes. But getting there via sail power in bad weather was a different story.

I wiped a raindrop—and a bead of sweat—from my forehead.

"We should lower the sails and shift to engine power," I said. "Before the wind gets too strong. I'm a decent sailor. But I'm not experienced enough to sail us back into the cove in a heavy storm."

Bess and George agreed. Working together, we quickly pulled in the sails and secured them in place. I sat at the *Sail Away*'s helm, Bess and George squished in next to me. I turned the key to start the engine.

It made a sputtering noise and died.

That was strange. I stared at the control panel and tried again.

Still nothing.

"What's wrong?" George asked.

I chewed my bottom lip and twisted the key another time.

Sputter, sputter, stop . . .

"The engine won't start," I answered, fear beginning to prickle up my spine. This wasn't the time or place for engine failure. I pushed the fear back down. The worst thing to do in a situation like this was panic. I turned the key again.

Nothing.

"Is it out of gas?" Bess asked.

I checked the fuel gauge and tapped it. "No. We have a full tank."

"Could it be the battery?" George asked.

"Doesn't seem to be," I said, peering at the control panel again. The depth finder and radio were both functional. "The other instrumentation is working."

I gave the key one last twist. This time, the engine didn't even sputter. But my heart did.

"The engine is just . . . dead," I said, swallowing hard. The storm intensified. Heavy raindrops smacked onto the deck and pinged against the mast. The boat heaved in the increasingly large waves.

"What are we going to do?" Bess asked, gripping

the edge of her seat as she looked at the darkening horizon. "Can we raise the sails again?"

A huge gust of wind blew and the boat listed heavily to one side. I struggled to keep my balance. "I don't think that's a good idea," I said. "The wind is getting too strong. I'm not sure I can control the boat under sail power. We need to radio for help. We're too far from shore to do anything else."

And, I thought but didn't say, the closest shore was nothing but jagged rocks. And the wind was blowing us in that direction. . . .

I hurried down the ladder into the cabin, trying not to fall over, and grabbed the emergency radio. Back on deck, I switched it on. Nothing happened. Not even a crackle of static. I tried turning the knob off and on again.

"Weird," I said.

"Is it broken?" Bess asked, her voice rising a pitch.

"I don't know," I said.

"Let me see it." George held out her hand. She turned a few knobs, frowning, then flipped the radio over. She pressed her fingers against the battery compartment, sliding the cover away with a click. The color drained from her cheeks. "Nancy," she said. "It isn't broken. There aren't any batteries." She spun the radio around so I could see the empty compartment.

"Megan would never send us out without a working radio," I said with a gulp. "There's no way she forgot to install batteries. *In a brand-new radio.*"

There was no way we were dealing with a prankster, either. I was sure of that now.

The rain intensified and the gusts grew stronger. A crack of thunder sounded.

"It's okay," I said, trying to stay calm. "We'll use our phones to call for help."

I grabbed my phone and tapped the screen, reading the display with horror: *No service.*

"Have you seen any cell towers around here?" I said.

George shook her head. "The reception is terrible at the resort, too."

"Let me see if I can find a signal." I maneuvered around the boat, gripping what I could for balance and holding my phone high in the air. Half a bar flickered onto the screen, then disappeared just as quickly. I extended my arm toward the boat's front deck and the half bar appeared again.

"I think I can get one up here!" I carefully stepped around the cabin and onto the slippery front deck, holding on to the mast as tight as I could with one hand for balance. I waved the phone around with the other. A full signal bar appeared. Then two. Yes!

I tried to tap out 911 with my thumb. But the phone kept moving each time the boat lurched. I shouted a command, but the wind drowned out my words.

I gripped the phone tight and tried again.

9—

1—

1—

Now all I needed to do was hit the send button!

But I couldn't angle the phone one-handed far enough to tap the bottom of the screen without dropping it. What now?

I'd have to let go of the mast: that was the only

solution. Just long enough to send the call. Shakily, I released my grip, planted my feet in a wide stance, and aimed my pointer finger at the phone.

"Nancy, be careful!" Bess cried out.

Suddenly a gust of heavy wind whipped past. The *Sail Away* spun and listed completely to one side. I grabbed for the mast, but it slipped from my wet fingers. My feet went out from under me. I fell sideways. My phone flew from my hand, skidded across the rain-slick deck, and sailed into the water.

I skidded along after it.

"No!" I yelled. Bess and George screamed. I reached for something to hold on to and stop myself from sliding. But there was nothing in sight. Through the rain I could see the edge of the boat, coming up fast.

And on the other side, the churning waters of Lake Champlain.

CHAPTER TEN

A Rescue Operation

AS MY BODY SLID TOWARD THE EDGE OF the boat, I scrabbled for something—anything—to stop me from going overboard. Just the deck, water on the other side, and wait . . . the front cleat!

I reached out and grabbed the metal cleat with both hands, gripping with all my might. My legs continued their slide, swinging off the boat so quickly I was sure the momentum would send me straight into the water. I gritted my teeth and held tight, trying to pull myself back onto the deck. But I couldn't get enough leverage.

A wave smacked against my face and I spit water. I

could feel my fingers slipping, losing their grip on the wet metal. I didn't know how much longer I could hold on. George's and Bess's shouts carried over the sounds of the wind, rain, and waves. I blinked and looked in their direction. George was standing alongside the cabin, holding one of the lines.

"Nancy, catch!" she yelled.

She swung the rope above her head like a lasso and threw the knotted end in my direction. It landed on the deck, a foot short of my reach. She pulled it back and tossed it again, coming up a few inches shy this time.

"Nancy, hang on!" Bess yelled as George coiled the rope.

She swung it hard.

The rope snaked through the air and landed right in front of the cleat. I grabbed the knot with one hand, then let go of the cleat completely and grabbed it with the other.

"Ready!" I said.

George pulled and I heaved my legs over the side of the boat, tumbling onto the deck. I held tight to the rope until I'd made it back to the cabin, where Bess extended her hand and guided me to safety.

"Nancy!" she said, her eyes wide with fear. "That was awful! I thought we were going to lose you in the water!"

"I'm okay," I said, taking a deep breath. "But we need to act fast. This storm is getting worse. And my phone is . . . gone."

There was only one thing left I could think of to do—and I hoped it would work.

I grabbed the flare gun from the emergency kit, hoping whoever had sabotaged the radio hadn't tampered with that, too. Shakily, I aimed the gun at the sky and pulled the trigger.

Breath held, I watched as the canister shot upward. After a few seconds it erupted into a bright orange flame, briefly illuminating the darkness. It was a beautiful sight. I let out a huge sigh of relief.

But my relief was short-lived. Lightning zigzagged across the black sky. A few moments later, a crack of thunder sounded. This was not what we needed.

Wind and rain were bad enough. An electrical storm was worse. Sitting in the middle of the lake on a tall-masted sailboat was the last place I wanted to be when lightning struck.

There was another flash of lightning, brighter than the last. I counted the seconds until I heard the thunder—twenty—and divided it by five. "The storm center is about four miles away," I said. "Which means it will be overhead in about twenty minutes."

"Twenty minutes?" Bess said, shivering.

I nodded. "The most important thing is to stay calm," I said, remembering everything I'd learned in my boater safety courses. "If we have to ride out this storm, the safest thing to do is to take shelter. George, help me drop anchor so we won't drift."

George and I pulled the metal anchor from its compartment and heaved it overboard. The chain securing it unspooled, *thwamp, thwamp, thwamp*. But when it reached the rope part of the anchor line, the chain suddenly detached with a whoosh. The rope snapped backward.

Empty.

We watched in horror as the anchor disappeared into the dark depths of the lake.

I picked up the severed rope and inspected the frayed end.

"What is it, Nancy?" George asked, even though I was pretty sure she already knew the answer.

I swallowed. Hard. "It's been cut."

Another gust of wind hit. The rain started coming down in sheets. I could hardly see two feet in front of myself. Bess whimpered.

"Come on," I said. "We need to get inside."

"And then what?" Bess said.

"And then we hope somebody saw our flare. Make sure your life jackets are secured," I said as we descended into the cabin.

We huddled together. The cabin seemed to grow smaller and more claustrophobic as the sky grew darker outside. I kept an eye on the weather and the position of the boat through the cabin's small porthole window. Not that I could see much through the rain. The boat lurched and rocked against the growing waves. Every minute felt like an hour.

"What if nobody saw the flare?" Bess said.

"Then we'll have to hope this storm disappears as quickly as it arrived," I said. "Or that Megan has already called to report us missing."

The boat listed again and we fell sideways. I made everyone check their life jackets a second time. We yanked the straps and double-checked the clips. Another bolt of lightning lit up the sky. The storm was getting closer.

And judging by the direction of our drift, we were getting closer to the rocky shoreline.

Suddenly there was a loud *clunk* outside. The boat jolted.

"What was that?" George said. "Did we hit something?"

"I don't know," I answered. "I sure hope not."

Another *clunk*. I bit back a scream.

A beam of light flashed across the porthole window.

"Oh no!" Bess exclaimed. "The lightning is right on top of us."

I pushed my face to the porthole window and peered outside, heart thumping. "Wait!" I said. "I don't think that was lightning. I'm going to get a better look."

"Nancy, be careful!" Bess said.

"I will."

I pushed the hatch open and climbed from the cabin into the blowing wind. Rain pelted my face. I shielded my eyes and searched for the source of the light. There it was! An aluminum fishing boat had pulled up next to the *Sail Away*. Ricky stood at the helm, wearing a bright yellow raincoat with the hood pulled tight over his head. He held up a rope.

"Hook up!" he shouted over the storm. "I'll tow you in!"

I scrambled across the deck, keeping low so I wouldn't fall again. Ricky threw me the rope. I tied it to the front cleat. When I was finished, I shimmied to the stern and gave Ricky the thumbs-up. He nodded back and started his engine. Another flash of lightning, followed by a clap of thunder—ten seconds between them now. The storm was only two miles away.

We had to hurry!

Ricky put his boat in drive and began to carefully—but quickly—tow us around the cove to the dock. We arrived sopping wet and shaken, but grateful to be alive. And off the water.

When she saw us pull up, Megan ran to the end of the dock through the rain as fast as her booted foot would allow.

"Nancy, Bess, George!" she said as we climbed shakily from the *Sail Away*. She deftly secured the boat. "I'm so relieved you're back. I've been worried sick. I tried to reach you and tell you about the storm when I saw the weather alert. These things can pop up quite suddenly here, without much warning. I was just getting ready to call the coast guard station in Burlington when Ricky called me to say he'd seen your flare from his house. I'm so glad you're okay! And Ricky, I can't thank you enough. Again."

Ricky nodded. "No problem, Miss Cho," he said.

"I've gotta go and tie up before the lightning is right on us."

"Yes, go!" Megan said, waving him away.

Ricky sped off. Megan led us back into the house, where she made hot chocolate while we changed into dry clothes. Her eyes radiated concern when we came back downstairs and sat at the kitchen table.

"What happened out there?" she said. "Why didn't you use the engine to come back?"

"We couldn't," I said. "It wouldn't start."

"It wouldn't start?" Megan said. "That doesn't make any sense. The tank was full. Everything was working just fine a couple of days ago."

I took a sip of hot chocolate and briefly closed my eyes. I couldn't imagine anything tasting better at this moment. My eyes flicked open and I met Megan's gaze. "Unfortunately, that wasn't the only thing that doesn't make sense," I said. "When we dropped anchor, we discovered the rope had been cut."

"Oh no." Megan's eyes widened.

"There's more," I said. "We tried to call for help.

But the emergency radio didn't work either. The batteries had been pulled out."

"I put the batteries in the radio myself and tested it yesterday." Megan swallowed hard. "I should have checked it again before you went out."

"It's not your fault," Bess said. "How could you know?"

"One thing I do know—clearly, I'm not being pranked," Megan said. "There's someone who doesn't want me—or my resort and club—here at all."

CHAPTER ELEVEN

~❧~

If You Don't Like the Weather

BEYOND THE KITCHEN WINDOW, THE clouds moved away. The sky shimmered bright blue. A perfect summer afternoon. It was almost as if the storm had never happened. Megan peered outside. "Typical Vermont," she said. "The locals say if you don't like the weather around here, wait five minutes. I wish I could say the same about everything else going on. How am I supposed to hold my opening celebration in two days?"

"Don't worry," I said with resolve. "We're going to get to the bottom of this."

"Nancy's right," George said. "We will. She's never left a case unsolved."

"Why don't we give that security footage another try?" I said. "What do you think, George?"

"I think this time, I'm not giving up," George answered.

"You three are the best," Megan said. "I guess I'd better call the sheriff again. I don't think he can chalk this up to pranksters anymore. Then I'm going to take a look at the boat."

Megan disappeared into the living room to make her phone call. Bess, George, and I moved next door to the lodge, where George parked herself in front of the computer at the front desk. She tapped a few keys and pulled up the software for the security system. Bess and I peered over her shoulder.

"What do you think is wrong with it?" Bess asked. "Has it been tampered with?"

"I'm not sure yet," George said. "Someone would

have needed access to this computer to mess with the footage. Or they'd have to be an expert hacker. It's more likely the equipment isn't set up properly, but I'll figure it out." Her mouth twisted to the side and she typed furiously.

I moved to one of the cushy sofas and balanced George's laptop on my knees. Bess sat next to me. Time to see what some internet sleuthing could tell me about the fire at the old resort. I couldn't shake the feeling that Megan's problems were directly tied to whatever had occurred back then.

First I googled *Gemstone Islands Resort*. Then I tried adding the word *fire*. I even threw in *Captain Stone* a couple of times for good measure.

Despite my best efforts, I couldn't find anything helpful. All I managed to track down were a few headlines from the local newspaper, the *Burnham Bugler*. But the articles themselves weren't available digitally.

I closed the computer and groaned.

Megan came inside, a towel slung over her

shoulder, sweat dripping from her forehead. She sat opposite me and dabbed away the sweat with her towel.

"How is the boat?" I asked hopefully.

Megan shrugged. "I couldn't find anything wrong with the engine. Well, except for the fact that it won't start."

"What about the sheriff?" Bess asked.

"He's on his way," Megan said. "He finally agrees that somebody is trying to sabotage my grand opening. He should be here soon. I'm really sorry your visit has turned into such a disaster!" She dropped her head into her hands.

"Sorry!?" I exclaimed. "You haven't done anything wrong."

"Exactly," Bess said. "The only one to blame is whoever is behind all this!"

"But who?" Megan said.

"Let's see," I said. "Are you sure Mr. Plath wouldn't resort to dirty tricks to disrupt your opening? And if not Mr. Plath, can you think of anyone else?"

"I still don't feel like Mr. Plath would do this," Megan answered. "Or maybe I don't *want* to feel like he'd do this. But anyone else? Beats me. I've run into a few people who are skeptical that I can make a go of it. But most of the locals I've met are pretty excited to see this area revived."

"What do you mean people are skeptical that you can make a go of it?" I asked.

"Oh, there have been all sorts of things that have started and stopped on this property over the years since the old resort burned down. A half-built golf course. A proposed condominium development that went bankrupt and left a bunch of investors holding the bag." Megan paused and took a deep breath. "Every time something failed, the locals said it was because Captain Stone didn't approve."

George tapped a few keys and said, "Aha!"

Bess, Megan, and I spun to face her.

"Did you get the video to work, George?" Bess said.

George's shoulders drooped. "No. I thought I had. But no."

She began typing again, an even more determined look on her face.

"Megan, what do you know about the fire at the old resort?" I asked.

"Not much," she answered. "Seems to be a touchy subject around here. As I mentioned before, there might have been suspicious circumstances surrounding it. Nobody knew for certain what caused it. So of course they blamed . . ."

"Captain Stone," Bess and I said in unison.

"You got it," Megan said.

There was a bump overhead. A few minutes later, Owen came down the stairs wearing a frustrated look—and a smudge of blue paint—on his face. He startled when he noticed us sitting in the great room.

"Oh!" he said.

"Everything okay?" Megan asked.

"Not exactly," he said. "Got my foot twisted in the ladder upstairs and fell off."

"Oh no," Megan said. "Are you hurt?"

Owen shook his head. "Nope," he said. "I'm fine. But I wouldn't have gotten all twisted up if I had my favorite paintbrush. The one that reaches into all the corners. Not the same using the big one."

"What happened to your favorite paintbrush?" Bess said, eyebrow quirked.

"Went missing yesterday," Owen said. "Along with my last can of paint. Had to go buy replacements today. And the hardware store was plum out of skinny paintbrushes."

"I'm sorry, Owen. I'll reimburse you for those," Megan said. "Just let me know what they cost, okay?" He nodded.

"Owen," I said. "I'm curious: Where exactly did your supplies go missing from?"

"Keep 'em out there under the porch," he said. "I mean, I did. Will be locking 'em in my truck from here on out. Don't know who would want an old paintbrush and a half-empty can of paint," he muttered, and headed toward the door. "Anyway, I'm all done for the day. See you tomorrow, Miss Cho."

"Bye, Owen," she said.

I watched him go. Owen might not know who would want his old paint supplies. But I was beginning to have an idea.

"You know," I said. "Something tells me the key to figuring out who's targeting your club, Megan, is learning more about what happened out here fifteen years ago. I didn't have much luck researching online. But I saw a library in town. Maybe they'd have old copies of the local paper there."

"Good idea," Bess said. "I'll come with you!"

There was a loud knock on the lodge's main door.

"Miss Cho?" a deep voice said. A man poked his head inside.

"Come on in," Megan said. A burly uniformed man with a dark mustache walked into the foyer. "Thanks for coming, Sheriff Parker," Megan said. She introduced each of us. He responded with a smile and tip of his hat.

"I'm sorry to hear about all the trouble out here

and for not taking you seriously before, Miss Cho," he said. "Mind if I have a look around?"

"Of course not. Let's hit the dock first." She glanced back over her shoulder as she walked out the door. "Car keys are on the kitchen table if you'd like to drive into town while I chat with Sheriff Parker."

"Sounds like a plan," I said, standing. "How's it going, George?"

George glanced up from the computer screen, still typing. "Making progress," she said. "Hopefully I can fix this by the time you get back."

I hoped so too.

CHAPTER TWELVE

~❧~

The Fire

THE ONLY SIGN OF THE MIDDAY STORM that had nearly drowned us earlier was a few deep puddles. Bess and I dodged them as we drove Megan's car into town. As we navigated past the field of wildflowers, a thought occurred to me.

"Mr. Plath's house is back that way, right?" I said.

"Yeah," Bess said. "Why?"

"I think we should pay him a quick visit." I did a three-point turn and headed in the other direction, past Megan's property, and slowed in front of a tree-lined gravel driveway. A wrought-iron mailbox marked PLATH sat at the end.

"Are you sure about this?" Bess said nervously as I pulled into the driveway. "Mr. Plath didn't strike me as the sort of person who appreciates unexpected visitors."

"That's exactly why we're showing up," I said. "I want to catch him off guard and ask him a few questions before he's had time to contemplate his answers."

"What if he's the person who's doing this?" Bess said. "Somebody has already tried to drown us once!"

"But what if he isn't? He may have seen something. Either way, I want to talk to him. And maybe have a look around . . ."

We parked in front of Mr. Plath's home, a small log cabin that faced the water. Solar panels lined the roof. Tidy rows of bright flowers were planted alongside the stone walkway that led to the front door. I got out of the car and Bess reluctantly followed.

"I still don't think this is a good idea," she said.

I rapped my knuckles lightly on the door. "Mr. Plath?" I called.

Nobody answered. I knocked again, a bit louder. "Mr. Plath?"

Silence.

"I don't think he's home," Bess said. "We should go."

"Or," I said, "maybe we should have a quick look around."

"Nancy, really?" Bess said, giving me a concerned look. "Isn't that trespassing?"

"I'm not saying we'll go inside," I answered. "Let's just walk around back. We can see if he's here somewhere and didn't hear us. That's all. That doesn't meet the legal requirements of trespassing, I don't think."

Bess rolled her eyes and groaned. "You have an answer for everything, don't you?"

"I try," I said with a smirk.

We skirted the edge of the house, walking across the neatly mown grass that led to the lakefront. I called out Mr. Plath's name a few more times as we went. There was nothing particularly remarkable to see on his property, except for the fact that Mr. Plath was an excellent gardener. His backyard featured three raised garden beds filled with colorful flowers and vegetables. As gruff as Mr. Plath could be, I couldn't help but think that someone who lovingly grew their own tomatoes was probably not the sort to vandalize boats. It didn't add up.

But then, nothing about this case was adding up.

Not yet.

"He doesn't seem to be here," I said. "Let's head to the library before they close."

Bess nodded in agreement. "Finally!"

But as we walked back to the car, something caught my eye. A small shed sat at the edge of Mr. Plath's property, tucked among the trees. I detoured to have a look. The door was cracked just a bit, so I poked my head inside. It took a moment for my eyes to adjust to the dim light. But when they did, I gasped.

"Bess!" I said in a loud whisper. "You're not going to believe this."

She hurried over. "What is it?"

I pushed the door open and pointed.

There, amid the shovels, garden spades, and rakes, was a stack of bright orange life jackets.

"I don't know, Nancy," she said, chewing her bottom lip. "That doesn't necessarily prove anything. Those life jackets are pretty generic."

"Except, look a little closer." I pointed again at the bottom of the life jackets, where *Gemstone Islands Eco-Resort* had been written in black marker.

"Oh!" Bess said, eyes widening. "That's evidence. We should call Megan. The sheriff!"

We stood at the door for a moment, looking at what we'd found. Just then a loud voice cut through the air.

"What are you two interlopers doing in my shed?"

Bess and I jolted and spun around. The shed door banged shut behind us. Bess gripped my arm. I pasted a friendly smile on my face.

Mr. Plath came up the lawn, scowling. He stopped and leaned on his cane. His very *thick* cane. I couldn't help but note that it would make an excellent weapon, if someone was so inclined to use it that way.

"I asked you a question," he said. "What are you two doing in my shed?"

I squared my shoulders. "Sorry, we were just looking for you, Mr. Plath," I said.

"And you thought you'd find me in the shed?" Mr. Plath narrowed his eyes in suspicion.

"We apologize," Bess said. "We didn't mean to disturb you."

"Then what did you come here for?" he asked. "Does this have something to do with your friend's resort?"

"Actually, yes," I said. "There's been some . . . trouble down there."

"Oh? I could have told you that. The resort *is* trouble. We don't need a bunch of tourists and boaters coming out here to disturb the wildlife and trample all over the fields and beaches," he grumbled.

"Is that why you took Megan's life jackets?" I asked, keeping my tone and face neutral. Bess quivered slightly beside me.

"Took 'em?" Mr. Plath huffed. "I found those things washed up on my beach. Put them in the shed for safekeeping. You can take them back, if you'd like. And tell your friend to be more careful with her stuff!"

He spun around and stomped toward the house. Bess and I grabbed the life jackets from the shed. When we came back out, Mr. Plath was standing right there. I nearly dropped my armload of life jackets. Mr. Plath held a white trash bag, stuffed full. He shoved it toward me with a scowl, and the items inside rattled.

"You can also tell your friend to quit throwing her garbage in the lake," he said. "Found this junk washed up alongside her life jackets. Some environmentalist she is!"

Mr. Plath dropped the garbage bag at my feet and tottered back toward the house.

"Wait!" I said.

Mr. Plath spun around. "Yes?"

"I have another question," I said.

Bess stiffened next to me. "What are you doing, Nancy?" she whispered. "Just let him go. . . ."

I couldn't do that. "We saw you out digging in the field yesterday," I continued. "I'm curious: Why?"

"Hmph. Darn right I was digging," Mr. Plath said. "Getting rid of the thistles. It's an invasive species. Let 'em take over and they crowd out all the desirable plants. Kind of like tourists!"

With that, he clomped up his front steps and went inside. The door slammed shut behind him. Bess and I quickly loaded the life jackets and garbage bag into the trunk, got back into the car, and headed out of there.

"Wow," Bess said as we drove away. "He really dislikes Megan's resort. And he sure is grumpy about it! Seems awfully suspicious."

"He definitely has strong feelings," I answered. "But something's bugging me about what he said back there."

"Do you think he was lying about finding the life jackets?" Bess asked.

"Hmm, could be," I said. "That's not what's bothering me, though."

"What is it, then?" Bess asked.

"The garbage," I said.

"What about it?"

"You heard Megan talking about finding trash in the hunting cabins. How upset she was. Megan has always been the sort of person who takes the time to pick up other people's trash," I said. "I don't see her chucking her own into the lake. It doesn't make sense."

"You're right," Bess remarked. "It doesn't make sense. But who's been throwing Megan's things in the lake, then?"

"Figure that out," I said, "and I'm quite certain we'll figure out who's behind all the sabotage."

We arrived in the village of Burnham. Like GIGS, the town library was located in a renovated Victorian house situated along the town square. The building was red with bright white trim. Colorful flower baskets hung from the porch. Bess and I pulled up right in front, parked the car, and got out.

We climbed the porch steps and went inside. I glanced around. From what I could see, the library seemed to occupy every room of the house. There were stacks upon stacks of old tomes lining the library's floor-to-ceiling shelves. Dust motes danced in the beams of sunlight streaming in from the tall windows. The front desk sat empty.

"Wow. I'm not even sure where to start," I said, wishing I had time to get a book and read. On a normal day, I could've spent hours in a place like this. I could only imagine what sorts of interesting old books were tucked away on these shelves!

Bess and I walked into the first room. A chandelier hung from the ceiling and a hutch was built into the far wall. Once upon a time, I imagined, this had been the home's formal dining room. Only now, instead of fancy plates, the hutch was filled with gardening guides and cookbooks.

We continued on to a small parlor that was outfitted with a pair of high-backed sofas and old artwork. A shiny glass case housed an antique clothing display filled with frilly lace dresses and faded leather shoes. Bess wandered toward it.

"We don't have time," I said, shaking my head.

Bess sighed and we carried on, moving to the next room.

A woman, book in hand, peered from behind one of the shelves as we entered. She was in her late thirties or early forties, with curly brown hair pulled into a ponytail and silver wire-rimmed glasses perched at the tip of her nose.

"Oh!" she said, shelving her book and pushing her glasses into place. "I'm sorry, I didn't hear you come in. I'm Mrs. Sofferman, the librarian. Can I help you find anything?" She smiled.

"Actually, yes," I said. "Thank you! We wondered if you might have old editions of the *Burnham Bugler* here. We can't seem to find anything online going back any further than ten years."

"Sure we do," Mrs. Sofferman said. "Exactly how far back do you need to go?"

"Fifteen years ought to do it," I answered.

"We have the last *fifty* years archived on microfiche, so that shouldn't be a problem. Follow me." The librarian led us through the stacks, up a set of creaky hardwood stairs covered with a faded green runner, and into a small turreted room. A clunky monitor that looked like a vintage computer, minus the keyboard, sat on a small table next to a set of filing cabinets.

"Have you ever used a microfiche machine?" she asked.

"Long time ago," I said. "Might need a refresher." I tried to imagine George's face if she saw this contraption. It looked like something straight out of technology's dark ages—which as far as George is concerned, is anything before 2010.

"It's easy," Mrs. Sofferman said. She opened a filing cabinet drawer and pulled out a small box. "All the film in here is labeled by date," she explained. "We'll use this one from April 1985 as an example."

Bess and I leaned in, intrigued, as Mrs. Sofferman opened the box and removed a roll of film. Actual film! I really wished George was here to see this. Hopefully she was making progress on the security video.

The librarian placed the film on a spool to the left

of the monitor, then threaded it beneath a glass plate and hooked it to an empty spool on the other side. She pushed a button and the monitor lit up. She pressed another button. The film zipped across the glass plate and newspaper articles zoomed across the screen.

"You control the scrolling speed with these buttons," she said, demonstrating. "Unfortunately, it's not quite like an internet search—you actually have to go through every date to find what you're looking for."

"Wow," Bess said. "Can you imagine George's face if she saw this?"

"I was thinking the same thing," I said with a grin. "She'd probably self-implode."

"I should introduce you to our old card-catalog system next," Mrs. Sofferman said. "We still have it up in the attic. It used *actual cards*!"

Bess and I laughed.

Mrs. Sofferman unspooled the film and put it away. "Anyway, that's how the microfiche works! Any questions?"

"No, thank you," I said. "This is perfect."

"Okay, I'll leave you to it." She smiled. "I'll be down at the desk if you need any help."

"Thanks!" I said.

Mrs. Sofferman headed back downstairs. I opened the filing cabinet and began sorting through the boxes. There were hundreds in here. Finally I found the box from the year of the fire. I popped it open and threaded the film as Mrs. Sofferman had demonstrated. Bess and I sat in front of the monitor.

I pressed the button and newspaper images streamed past. Ice-fishing derby winners, ski condition reports, a huge blizzard warning. And then the unmistakable image of a fiery blaze zipped by. I backed up and paused the film. Bess gasped. There, beneath a banner headline FIRE DESTROYS GEMSTONE ISLANDS RESORT, was a black-and-white photograph of the resort I'd seen in the picture at Charlotte's house. But this time, it was completely engulfed in flames.

"Wow," Bess said with a shudder. "That looks horrible. No wonder people don't like to talk about it."

I nodded and read the story.

FIRE INVESTIGATORS HAVEN'T
RULED OUT FOUL PLAY IN GEMSTONE
ISLANDS RESORT BLAZE;
BLIZZARD DERAILS INVESTIGATION

The state fire marshal announced today that the cause of the blaze that burned the popular Gemstone Islands Resort to the ground may be suspicious, after investigators found traces of an accelerant in the rubble. The fire, which is believed to have started in the living quarters, quickly engulfed the twenty-five-room resort, dining hall, and ballroom, destroying the entire property.

The resort was closed for the winter at the time of the fire, and the guest quarters were vacant. Resort caretakers Bob and Betsy Sensbach were not home when the blaze broke out. Investigators have confirmed that they were at the Top Notch restaurant in Stowe all evening, celebrat-

ing their anniversary. Mrs. Sensbach's sister, Judith Lawson, 19, was babysitting her nephew, one-year-old Ricky Sensbach, when the fire occurred. Young Ricky was rescued unharmed. Sadly, however, Ms. Lawson is presumed to have perished in the blaze. Further attempts to investigate and recover Ms. Lawson's remains have unfortunately been hampered by the recent nor'easter that dumped more than two feet of snow on the region. The investigation will resume in the spring.

Judith Lawson? I read the name again. I thought about Charlotte and her reluctance to talk about the fire. What she had to say about her husband and their "Judy" treasure hunting together. The redheaded girl who had disappeared from the family photographs.

"Oh, poor Charlotte," Bess said, clearly thinking the same thing. "I didn't realize her daughter died in the fire. That's terrible!"

"It is," I said. "No wonder she clammed up when I mentioned the fire."

"And why she seemed so sad remembering her kids sitting around the kitchen table . . ."

"Then there's Ricky. . . ." I thought again about the photograph in Charlotte's foyer of the young couple holding a baby. "It looks like his parents were the ones who managed the resort."

"And they must have lost everything in that fire," Bess said, shaking her head sadly. "What a tragedy."

A tragedy, for sure.

And maybe a motive, too.

CHAPTER THIRTEEN

The Survivor

BESS AND I READ A FEW MORE STORIES, until our eyes glazed over from the blur of newsprint zooming across the microfiche screen.

Ultimately, we learned that while the cause of the fire had never been fully determined, investigators couldn't find any concrete evidence that foul play was involved. The massive snowstorm had made it nearly impossible to conduct a full investigation. When the snow had finally disappeared in the spring, so had most of the evidence. The fire was ruled a tragic accident. The property went up for sale. Ricky and his parents moved to his dad's hometown in New Jersey, where they'd been ever since.

"I think we've found as much here as we can," I said, standing and cracking my neck. I could feel the beginning of a sunburn forming beneath my ponytail. I'd obviously missed a spot with the sunscreen when we'd gone sailing earlier . . . today? Wow, it wasn't even dinnertime yet, and I felt like I'd been awake for days. "Let's go."

Bess and I packed up the microfiche, switched off the machine, and went back downstairs. We found Mrs. Sofferman sitting at the front desk. She was stamping returned books and placing them on a metal cart.

"Hello!" she said. "Did you find everything you were looking for?"

"Some," I answered. "We still have questions, though."

"Maybe I can answer them," Mrs. Sofferman said. "We librarians are founts of knowledge, you know! We live for questions."

Finally, I'd found someone in this town who liked them!

"So, ask away," Mrs. Sofferman said.

"I'm Nancy and this is Bess. We're here visiting my friend Megan Cho," I said. "Megan's the one who rebuilt on the old Gemstone Islands Resort property, and we're interested in learning more about it. You don't happen to know anything about the fire that destroyed the old resort, do you?"

"Sure I do," Mrs. Sofferman answered. "A terrible tragedy. I was in college at the time, but I remember it well. Went to high school with Judy, actually."

"So you knew her?" I said.

"Couldn't help but know her. We were a pretty tight-knit class," she said. "Small town and all that. But unlike the rest of us, Judy always had one foot out the door, so to speak. Lots of us stuck around, got married, went to college nearby. Not Judy. She took off the day after we graduated to backpack across Europe. She was back home for the holidays when the fire occurred. Babysitting her little nephew. She loved that kid."

"Ricky?" Bess said.

"Yep, Ricky," Mrs. Sofferman answered. "Anyway,

I'd heard Judy was planning to attend college the next fall. Study movement therapy or something like that. She was very into New Agey kind of stuff. Started a yoga club at our school, in fact. I tried joining, but it wasn't for me. I fell on my head doing a downward dog." A sad smile crossed Mrs. Sofferman's face. "At least little Ricky survived. Such a good kid, too. He swings by here nearly every week to pick up books for his grandmother. She's one of our biggest patrons."

"About Ricky," I said. "It wasn't really clear in the stories. How did he survive? He was just a baby, right?"

"Well, nobody knows exactly how he made it out," Mrs. Sofferman said. "It was a miracle, really. He was a year old. His grandparents, Charlotte and Arthur, found him sitting in their mudroom in his pajamas after the fire broke out. The only words he said at the time were things like ma-ma and da-da. When he was asked how he got there, his answer was, 'Pa-rah.'"

"Pa-rah?" I said.

"Yep," Mrs. Sofferman said. "Pa-rah. So of course, people speculate that little Ricky was trying to say 'pirate.' And that the pirate was none other than the ghost of Captain Stone, who returned from the dead to rescue the boy. And others . . ."

"Yes?" I asked.

"Others like to say Captain Stone was the one who caused the fire in the first place. Some sort of revenge for building a resort on the site of his old tavern," she said.

"Why would Captain Stone even care that someone built there?" Bess said.

"Legend has it that's where Captain Stone spent most of his days, after his wife died in childbirth," Mrs. Sofferman said. "He spent the remainder of his life raising their daughter, tending bar, and spinning yarns about his exploits on the high seas during his early days. Had everyone convinced he'd pirated gold from sunken galleons and hidden it around his property."

"So that's why people still talk about a hidden treasure," I said, nodding.

"Ah-yup," Mrs. Sofferman said. "If you ask me, the captain probably invented the treasure stories to drum up business for his tavern. As for the fire, the most logical explanation is that ghosts do not start them—or rescue small children."

"How *was* Ricky rescued, then?" Bess asked. "He was so little. How did he get next door?"

"Likely walked over and let himself in. Nobody ever locks their doors around here," Mrs. Sofferman explained. "And Ricky was a precocious and athletic kid. People say he'd already figured out how to walk, climb from his crib, and open doors by the time he was a year old. Word has it he grew into quite the escape artist too—never met a childproof lock he couldn't foil or a tree he couldn't climb. Drove poor Betsy to distraction. Though in the end, I guess that's what saved him, so it's not all bad, right?"

"Right," I said.

"Any other questions?" Mrs. Sofferman asked.

"Actually, yes," I said. "I'd like to learn a little more about Captain Stone. Do you have any books or articles about him?"

"Absolutely!" Mrs. Sofferman said. "We have an entire book, in fact. He wrote an autobiography. It's not exactly the best-written book around, but it is one of our most popular."

"Really?" Bess said. "Why?"

"Because people think the captain left clues in it about the location of his treasure, of course," she answered. "Let me grab it for you."

Clues? About the treasure? *Hmmm, interesting . . .* Bess and I gave each other a look.

Mrs. Sofferman disappeared into the stacks. She returned empty-handed a few minutes later, wearing a perplexed expression on her face. "It wasn't there," she said. "I don't recall anyone checking it out recently. Let me have a look on the computer."

She walked behind the desk and tapped the keyboard. "Well, that's odd," she said, frowning.

"What is?" I asked.

"The book was checked out two months ago," Mrs. Sofferman said, still staring at the computer screen. "Never returned. Which is also strange, because she always returns books on time. . . . Can't believe I missed that," Mrs. Sofferman said, mostly to herself.

"Missed what?" I asked, sensing a clue.

"Oh, it's nothing," Mrs. Sofferman answered. "Just need to follow up with a late notice. Anyway, it looks like you're in luck. They have a copy at the library in Colchester. It's the next town over. They're closed today, but they'll be open in the morning at nine."

"Great," I said. "Thanks for all your help. I really appreciate it."

"Anytime," Mrs. Sofferman said.

"One more thing before we go," I said. "Bess had some questions about that cool antique clothing display back there in the parlor. She's really into fashion."

"I thought you said we didn't have—?" Bess started. I nudged her discreetly with my foot. "Oh, I mean, I did! Have questions!"

"Really? How wonderful!" Mrs. Sofferman said, coming around the desk, hands clasped together. "I curated that display myself. Vintage clothing is a passion of mine. Along with books, of course. Let's go have a look!"

Once Bess and the librarian had rounded the corner, out of sight, I slipped behind Mrs. Sofferman's desk. I tapped the computer keyboard and the screen lit up. Lucky for me, she was still logged in. I scrolled back to the digital card catalog for Captain Stone's autobiography. I quickly read the information and my eyebrows shot straight up.

The book had been checked out online and picked up curbside nearly two months ago, by the one person we'd met who claimed to have no interest in Captain Stone's treasure.

Charlotte Lawson.

"Charlotte?" Bess said as we climbed back into the car. "What do you make of that?"

"I'm not sure yet," I said. "She's definitely an avid reader."

"She did have a lot of books at her house," Bess agreed.

"Mostly romance novels, though," I said, thinking.

Bess said, "Not exactly the sort of person who

reads autobiographies of dead pirates, huh? Seems rather suspicious."

"It does," I said. "But . . ."

"But what?"

"I don't know," I answered. "Something still feels off. Why didn't she return the book? It sounds like she always returns her books on time. Why keep that one and draw attention to herself?"

"Maybe because she hasn't found the treasure yet?" Bess volunteered. "Or the right clue?"

"Could be," I said. "Still, she couldn't be the one who sabotaged the *Sail Away*. There's no way she'd be able to maneuver down the dock and to the stern of the boat in her wheelchair. Not to mention the top of the hiking trails to dig for treasure. Unless . . ."

"She had an accomplice," Bess said.

"Ricky?" we said in unison.

Ricky most definitely had a funny way of turning up whenever there was trouble. Megan stepping in the hole . . . the *Sail Away* sailing away . . . Bess, George, and I being stranded on the lake during the storm.

And then there was the dirt on his boots, clothes, face. The shovel by the house. It seemed clear he'd been out digging for something. . . .

"He seems so sweet, though," Bess said. "And Charlotte, too! It can't be them. I mean, I don't want it to be them!"

I'd run into enough seemingly "sweet" culprits to know that likeability didn't always equal innocence. And the only way to determine guilt was to follow *all* the clues, no matter where they led.

I just needed to find the rest of the clues. . . .

As we continued to drive, I spotted a stand just off the side of the road. At least twenty people were lined up around it, waiting. Another dozen or so were hanging out on the grass lawn, licking ice cream cones. I read the sign out front: FRESH MAPLE CREEMEES!

"That must be the Shack!" I said. "Want to stop and get ice cream for everyone? I know I think better on a full stomach!"

"Maple ice cream?" Bess said. "Don't need to ask me twice!"

I flicked the turn signal and pulled into the parking lot. The Shack was a small, white-painted building with a colorful awning that extended over the front window. Bess and I hopped into line. A few minutes later we were armed with four dishes of soft-serve ice cream to go in a cardboard tray. Bess spooned a bite into her mouth.

"This is delicious," she said around a mouthful of ice cream. "Even better than maple lattes, if you can believe it! Or, maybe as good. I'll probably need to conduct a few taste tests. Do you think George will mind if I eat hers, too?"

When we got back to the lodge, George barreled out the front door. And it wasn't to rescue her ice cream from Bess.

"Nancy!" she shouted, meeting the car as we rolled to a stop. I opened the door and stepped out. Bess followed with the tray of ice cream.

"What is it?" I asked.

"The security video," George exclaimed. "I got it to work! And you're not going to believe what's on it."

CHAPTER FOURTEEN

∾

To Catch a Pirate

WE HURRIED INTO THE LODGE. MEGAN WAS sitting on the edge of the front desk, anxiously bouncing her booted foot. Bess set the ice cream next to her. George plopped in front of the computer and tapped the keyboard. The screen sprang to life.

George was right. I couldn't believe my eyes.

"Is that . . . ?" I stared in shock. Bess leaned over my shoulder. Her jaw dropped.

"Yep, the one and only," George said.

"Can you rewind the video?" I asked.

"Of course." George clicked the mouse. I leaned in closer to get a better look.

It was nighttime, the first night of our stay. The scene was quiet and still, save for the gentle rippling of the water. Suddenly a grainy figure appeared and walked down the dimly lit dock. It was hard to make out the details. But one thing was clear: the grainy figure was wearing a long coat and three-cornered hat, like a sea captain. He was clutching something. A bag, maybe? It was hard to tell. The video wasn't great. The figure stopped at the *Sail Away*, glanced left and right, then climbed on board. After a few minutes, the figure reemerged. Next, he opened the storage locker, pulled out the life jackets, and chucked them into the water.

Then he ran out of the frame.

"Can you enhance the image at all?" I asked George.

She shook her head. "I've tried. That's as clear as it gets. Sorry."

"Well, one thing *is* clear," I said. "Somebody is doing their best to make themselves look like Captain Stone—and derail Megan's grand opening in the process."

"Do you think it's Mr. Plath?" Bess asked. "He sure got mad when we stopped by his place today. And he definitely doesn't want tourists down here."

"You went to see Mr. Plath?" George asked.

"Yes," I said. "And I don't think it's him. The person in that video was moving a bit too fast. Also, why would Mr. Plath bother throwing the life jackets into the water, just to pick them up later and put them in his shed?"

"Wait, Mr. Plath has my life jackets?" Megan asked, a hint of annoyance in her voice. "What is he doing with them?"

"Yes, he did have them," I said. "Bess and I got them back. They're in the car. Sorry, with all the excitement I forgot! Mr. Plath said they washed up in the cove. In fact, come with me. . . ."

I led Megan, Bess, and George outside to Megan's parked car. I popped the trunk and pulled out the garbage bag. The contents jangled inside.

"What is that?" Megan said.

"Some things Mr. Plath said you threw in the lake.

He told us they washed up on his beach and he bagged them to dispose of." I rifled through the bag.

"That *I* threw in the lake?" Megan exclaimed. "I'd never do that!"

"I know," I said. "That's exactly what made me suspicious. . . ."

I reached into the bag and set an empty paint can on the ground. Then a paintbrush. And then I found what I was looking for. I held an empty plastic bag in the air.

"You might want to call the sheriff back," I said. "Tell him to check the *Sail Away*'s engine for traces of sugar."

"Sugar?" Bess said.

"Yep," I said with a satisfied smile. "Sugar may be great in ice cream, but it will kill an engine."

George looked me up and down. "You've solved it, haven't you?" she said. "You know what this is about. Are you going to fill us in?"

"I have a theory," I said. "But I'm not a hundred percent sure yet. There are a few more things I need to investigate. So . . . who wants to stake out Pirate's Perch with me tonight?"

George, Bess, and I set up our hiding spot in the trees just off the path to Pirate's Perch. The sun had set and the air had cooled. Fortunately, we had a thick picnic blanket to sit on, sleeping bags, and a thermos filled with hot chocolate. An owl hooted in the distance. It was a plaintive and lonesome sound. Bess scooted a bit closer to me and George.

"It's kind of creepy out here," she said, glancing around.

"Remember, like I said before—it's just nature," I whispered. "Nothing to worry about."

But I shivered a little. It was cold, and I had no idea how long we'd have to wait. Or what would happen if I was wrong. All I could hope was that the "captain" was under some sort of pressure to speed up the search for the treasure, since the efforts to stop Megan's opening weren't exactly working.

George pulled out her phone and tapped the screen.

"Ugh, no cell signal either. There's nothing to do." She leaned back on her sleeping bag with a groan.

The minutes melted away and the full moon rose higher in the sky. Before I knew it, George and Bess had both fallen asleep. I could hardly keep my eyes open either. George began to snore softly.

Then I heard other sounds: *crunch, crunch, scrape, scrape, scrape . . .*

I sat up straight and gave George a little poke. She snorted and rolled onto her side. I tried Bess next. But she was completely out, face buried in the crook of her elbow.

Scrape, scrape, scrape . . .

I decided to check things out on my own. If I needed help, I would shout back to George and Bess. I crept from behind the trees slowly and softly, taking care not to crunch the leaves and twigs beneath my feet.

Scrape, thump, scrape, thump . . .

I reached the edge of the trail and stopped short.

There, by the patch of pine trees, stood the cloaked figure of "Captain Stone." A shovel flew into the air, metal tip glinting. Then it swung downward and the shovel slammed into the dirt. I tried to make out the captain's face—see if my theory was correct—but it was hidden beneath a three-cornered hat.

I crept closer for a better look.

Closer . . .

Closer . . .

Closer . . .

I was almost there, when . . .

Snap!

A twig cracked beneath my feet.

I froze.

Captain Stone stopped digging and stood up straight.

I held my breath and tried not to make another sound. But it was too late.

Captain Stone spun around and took off. I immediately gave chase. I followed the captain's billowing coattails as they disappeared into the woods.

"George! Bess!" I shouted. There was no time to go back and get them.

The captain took a quick glance back at me and ran even faster, dodging around rocks and downed branches with ease, not seeming to tire at all. I struggled to keep up. Clearly, the captain was very familiar with these woods. My breathing grew heavy as we ran farther and farther away from the main path. The forest grew denser. The sky grew darker as clouds slipped across the moon like ghosts.

I paused a moment to catch my breath and looked around.

I had no idea where I was anymore.

Somewhere high in the branches overhead a bird squawked. There was rustling in the leaves nearby. Not the captain, who was still running up ahead. An animal? Fear snaked its way up my spine. I shook it off. There wasn't time for that, because the captain was getting away!

I broke into a sprint, struggling to keep up. The captain dodged left, then right, then right again. I stumbled over a tree stump and nearly fell. I wasn't sure how long I could keep this up. Where on earth was the captain taking me?

Suddenly the landscape changed. The trail opened again. I slowed and took stock of my surroundings. We had run in a complete circle. We were back on the path to Pirate's Perch!

The captain stood ten feet away, leaning on the shovel, head bowed and breathing heavily. It seemed I wasn't the only one who'd grown tired running through the woods.

"I just want to talk to you," I said, inching my way forward. "That's all. . . ."

I took another cautious step.

And another.

"Stop!" the captain growled, raising the shovel menacingly.

I froze as a cloud drifted across the moon, plunging the forest into darkness. An eerie silence filled the air. I was acutely aware of my own breath. And the captain's.

My eyes adjusted to the dark and I took one more slow step, hands raised and palms out. "It's okay . . . ," I said in a calming voice.

The shovel swung toward me.

I reached out to stop it. But before I could, something else swung through the air and thwacked the captain's wrist, knocking the shovel to the ground. The captain crumpled next to it with a howl. The clouds shifted again, the moonlight illuminating another figure standing over the captain, scowling. My eyes widened.

"Mr.—" I began.

I was interrupted by the sounds of footsteps, branches rustling, and twigs snapping. George and Bess ran up next to me, breathless.

"*Mr. Plath?*" George said, finishing my sentence. Her eyes darted from me, to the captain curled on the ground, to Megan's grumpy neighbor standing there, the cane he'd used to knock the shovel from the captain's hand still hovering midair.

"Ah-yup," Mr. Plath said with his usual grumble. He lowered the cane and leaned on it. A pair of binoculars swung from his neck.

"What are you doing out here?" George continued as she gaped at the scene.

"I could ask the same of you!" Mr. Plath huffed. "I came out here to search for whip-poor-wills, heard the commotion, and saw this one here getting ready to swing a shovel at your friend." He pointed at the captain, still cowering on the ground. "Now, what in the devil is going on?"

"You caught the captain's ghost?" Bess said, leaning forward to get a better look. There was still a crease in her cheek from falling asleep on it. She rubbed her face and blinked.

"That's no captain," I answered. "But you could say there is something of a ghost roaming these woods."

At that, the "captain" tilted his—no, *her*—head up. Tears streamed down both cheeks. The hat fell from her head and red curls sprang loose around her shoulders.

"I'm so sorry," she said. "I wasn't trying to hurt anyone. I only wanted to scare you all away. Just long enough that I could finish my search. For the treasure. I had to do something, you know. To make up for the awful mess I'd made." She lowered her face into her hands and sobbed.

"Wait, I'm confused," George said. "Who is she? I've never seen her."

Before I could answer, Mr. Plath's mouth opened.

"Well I'll be," he said, eyes wide. "It's been some years now, but I'd know that face anywhere. Hello, *Judy*."

CHAPTER FIFTEEN

~❧~

The Ghost of Fires Past

"I CAN'T BELIEVE CAPTAIN STONE WAS Ricky's aunt, and she's been alive this whole time," Bess said, taking a sip of her coffee. It had been a long night, between Sheriff Parker arriving to take Judy into custody and the rest of us answering his many questions. We all needed caffeine. Lots of it. Even Jimmy Chew looked exhausted, curled on his bed in the corner.

"I still don't understand how you figured out it was her," George said.

"I didn't at first," I said. "But I started to get suspicious when I read that old newspaper article saying that Judy was 'presumed' dead. And then I thought about the yoga pants and pink T-shirt you'd found in one of the old hunting cabins, Megan. I pieced that together with what Mrs. Sofferman told us about Judy and the yoga club in high school."

"Wow," Bess said. "I totally missed that!"

"And then I thought about the missing library book by Captain Stone," I continued. "The one that had been checked out online, picked up curbside, and never returned. Very few people would have known how to check out a book using Charlotte's personal information."

"But her daughter would," Megan said.

"Exactly," I answered.

"And of course, once I saw the video George recovered, most of my suspicions were confirmed. Nice job, George," I said. George beamed.

"Wow. Poor Charlotte and Ricky." Megan shook her head. "They must be stunned. I still don't entirely understand why Judy pretended to be dead all these years."

I blew on my coffee, took a sip, and set the mug on the kitchen table. Once she'd been caught, Judy had readily—make that eagerly—confessed everything to me, Bess, George, and a very surprised Mr. Plath.

"She didn't really plan it that way," I recounted to Megan. "Judy was only nineteen at the time of the fire. Arthur—Judy's dad—was a huge believer in Captain Stone's treasure. She'd heard all these stories about Captain Stone growing up. How his ghost roamed the property. That he'd buried treasure somewhere nearby. So, the night of the fire, she was babysitting Ricky. Her older sister, Betsy, and brother-in-law, Bob, were out to dinner. She'd just put Ricky to bed in his crib when she came up with an idea: she'd hold a seance and try to summon the ghost of Captain Stone. Then she could ask him where he'd buried the treasure. She took the three-cornered hat from the display in the resort's dining room and put that on, along with one of Bob's long overcoats. Then she lit a bunch of candles in the living room and tried to communicate with the captain via Ouija board."

"But nothing happened, of course," George said. "Because there's no such thing as ghosts."

"Right," I said. "Nothing happened . . . except for the fact that Judy fell asleep."

"And accidentally kicked over one of the candles," Bess continued.

I nodded. "Starting the fire. Her first thought was to get Ricky out of there. She grabbed him from his crib and dashed to her parents' house. As she was running, the resort erupted in flames behind her. Apparently, they'd been doing some renovations during the closed season, and there were paint thinners and other chemicals scattered around the property that accelerated the fire. She set Ricky inside her parents' door, still wearing that hat and overcoat."

"So that's why Ricky said 'pa-rah' when everyone asked how he got to his grandparents' house. He *was* saying 'pirate'! Because Judy was dressed up like one," Bess said.

"Exactly," I said. "After Judy put Ricky safely inside, she ran back toward the resort, hoping she could do something to stop the fire before it spread even more."

"But it was too late," George said.

"It was too late," I repeated. "She heard the sirens and fire engines coming. And in that moment, she panicked and ran. When she discovered the next morning that the resort had been completely destroyed, she was consumed with guilt. And scared she'd be blamed. The fire had been her fault, after all. She left town, traveled around, and worked a bunch of odd jobs. She always figured she'd come back and try to explain. But the longer she was gone, the harder it got."

"Wow," said Megan. "I actually feel a bit sorry for her. I mean, not totally—she could have killed all of you on the boat! But it's still sad. She was just a kid herself, really, when the fire occurred."

I nodded. "It is sad. After her dad passed away a few months back, she was gutted and wanted to come home. But she worried about being held liable for the fire at the resort. So when she snuck back into town, she decided to find Captain Stone's treasure in hopes that it would cover the losses and make up for what she'd done."

"She really did believe in the treasure?" Megan asked.

"Yes, she did," I said. "She remembered her dad's old stories. The maps they used to draw. The hints that were supposedly hidden in Captain Stone's autobiography. She checked the book out of the library remotely under her mom's name to look for clues."

"And apparently, she found one," Bess piped up.

"Yep," I said. "That's why she was digging up by the perch. She still had the old coat and hat from the night of the fire. She figured it would make a good disguise. Plus, it would have the added bonus of scaring away people—like Melina—who might see her out there. Her plan was working out pretty well. But then . . ."

"I got ready to open the resort and club," Megan said.

"Exactly," I said. "Suddenly there were going to be a lot more people around—and it was going to be a lot more difficult to dig for treasure undetected. Especially once Charlotte agreed to let you use the trails up by Pirate's Perch."

"So she started sabotaging Megan's club to scare her and delay the resort's opening," George said.

"She will be facing charges for that," I said. "Especially for tampering with the boat—someone really could have been hurt. But I do think she's truly sorry and didn't mean to cause any harm."

"Let me get this straight, though," George said. "The entire time she's been searching for the treasure, she's just been *living* by herself in the woods?"

"Yeah, I mean, how? You know . . . ," Bess said, wrinkling her nose, "there aren't any bathrooms. Or stores!"

"She apparently set up a campsite that was hidden off the path," I explained. "Built her own latrine, bathed in the lake, caught fish at night, and foraged for wild nuts and berries. And when there was heavy rain or wind, she'd take shelter in one of the old hunting cabins. Like her nephew, Ricky, she knows the land well and is an experienced camper."

"What about the treasure?" George asked. "She never did tell us why she thought it was up at the perch. Do you think there's something up there?"

"Funny you should ask," I said. "I called Mrs. Sofferman at the library this morning to find out about getting that other copy of Captain Stone's autobiography. . . ."

Just then there was a knock on the door. Megan opened it. Mrs. Sofferman stood on the other side, holding a copy of *My View from the Perch: The Life of Captain Stone*.

"Hi, Nancy!" she said. "I picked the book up from the Colchester branch during my coffee break and thought I'd go ahead and swing it by, before I went back to work." She stepped inside and handed me the book. She craned her neck and looked around. "Heard you had some excitement out here last night, too . . ."

I had to grin. Burnham wasn't all that different from River Heights. Word sure does get around quickly in a small town. I think it's safe to say that the book delivery wasn't the *only* reason Mrs. Sofferman decided to pop by.

"Yeah, you could say that," I answered.

"Can't believe Judy survived that fire and that she's been back in town for a couple of months," she said. "And that you figured all that out!"

"She is Nancy Drew," Bess said with a grin. "It's what she does!"

"I couldn't have done it without my friends," I answered. "Or a good librarian!"

Mrs. Sofferman blushed. "Anyway, you must be Megan," she said, and held out her hand. Megan shook it. "The property looks fabulous. You've really cleaned it up out here. Congratulations! I'll be back for the opening celebration tomorrow to check it out. And I'd love to get some information on joining the club. I haven't sailed in ages!"

"Wonderful," Megan said. "I'll look forward to seeing you!"

Mrs. Sofferman wished us all a great day, then excused herself to return to the library. "Always more books to shelve and questions to answer!" she said on the way out.

I moved to the sofa in the living room, taking my coffee mug with me, and flipped open the book. The history of Captain Stone and the Gemstone property was quite fascinating, even if it wasn't particularly ghostly. Captain Richard Stone had settled here after serving in the Revolutionary War. He'd actually fought alongside General George Washington. At one point, he'd owned the entire peninsula, and he ran a small tavern where Megan's lodge now sat. He loved the sea and boasted of the "riches" he'd accumulated sailing them.

But Captain Stone's greatest love was his wife, Elizabeth, who had died giving birth to their only child. He never remarried and spent the remainder of his days running his small tavern. I flipped the page to a portrait of Mrs. Stone, and a little rush of adrenaline coursed through my veins—that very satisfying feeling when I've solved another mystery.

The next page featured a hand-drawn rendering of Mrs. Stone's grave marker. In the background was the view from Pirate's Perch. When I read the grave's inscription, I immediately understood why Judy had been digging up there.

For at day's end, what is life's measure?
'Tis love that is the greatest treasure!

Judy had miscalculated one very important part of the clue, though.

George walked into the living area and assessed my grinning face. "Why do you look like the cat that just ate the canary?"

"Or one who has just discovered another case," Bess said, folding her arms across her chest.

I closed the book and stood. "Not another case," I

said. "But we do have one more thing on the agenda today."

"I hope you're about to say maple creemees," Bess said.

"Nope," I answered. "Even better. We have a hidden treasure to find!"

CHAPTER SIXTEEN

The Greatest Treasure

CHARLOTTE ANSWERED THE DOOR, DARK circles beneath her reddened eyes. "Another pie?" she said when she spotted me, Bess, George, and Megan standing there. "You're sweet to come by. But we haven't quite finished the last one yet."

I shook my head. "No, but do you mind if we come in for a few minutes?"

"Of course not," Charlotte said. "But it's been a really long day already. Not sure how much we're up for chatting here. I'm so glad to have my Judy home, but I sure wish it hadn't been like this." She blinked back tears and glanced at Megan standing behind me.

"I'm sorry for the trouble she's caused you, Megan," Charlotte said.

Megan reached out and touched Charlotte's hand. "I know," Megan said. "And I know Judy didn't mean to hurt anyone. We're still neighbors and friends. Everything will be okay."

"Thank you," Charlotte said softly. She backed her wheelchair up, making room for us to enter. "Come in. Have a seat, if you'd like."

We followed Charlotte into the living area. My friends settled into chairs, but I walked past them, stopping in front of the portrait of Charlotte's ancestor. My palms tingled with excitement.

"Charlotte," I said over my shoulder, "you didn't mention that Elizabeth was married to Captain Richard Stone."

"Wait!" Bess said. "Elizabeth *Stone* is your great-great-great-whatever-it-was-grandmother? That means you're a descendant of Captain Stone, too?"

Charlotte took a deep breath. "Yes, I am," she said. "Ricky is named after him, in fact. And my daughter Betsy is named after Elizabeth."

"Wow, why didn't you tell us?" George said.

"Well, you didn't ask," Charlotte said. "And to be honest, I didn't really feel like it. You've seen firsthand what all that talk about a treasure that doesn't exist has done to my family."

"Well," I said. "About that . . ."

I pulled a small bottle and cotton ball from my pocket.

"What are you doing, Nancy?" Megan said.

"Do you mind if I try something, Charlotte?" I asked. Concern crossed her wrinkled face. "Don't worry. I promise I won't touch the painting," I added quickly.

"Okay," Charlotte said, raising an eyebrow and rolling closer to me. Megan, Bess, and George got up and stood behind her.

Just then the door was flung open and Ricky clomped in, once again with mud caked all over his boots. He began walking toward us. "What's going on?" he said.

"Ricky, stop right there!" Charlotte pointed at the tracks he was leaving on the floor.

"Sorry," he said, cheeks flushing. "I forgot! Again."

Charlotte looked him up and down, exasperated. "What on earth have you been doing out there that's getting you so muddy, anyway?"

Ricky glanced between us. "Well, I guess it's silly to keep it a secret anymore, because I'm almost done. I've been leveling the slope out back for you, Nana. So you can get down to the lake in your chair when I'm not around to help."

The exasperation on Charlotte's face washed away and she smiled broadly. "Oh, my sweet boy," she said. "What am I going to do with you? Come here and give me a hug. But take your boots off first!"

Ricky left his boots at the door and gave Charlotte a loving hug. Then he regarded us again, clustered around the painting of his great-great-something-grandmother.

"What are you all doing in front of that old picture?" he asked.

"Not sure yet," Charlotte said. "Nancy has something she wants to show us."

I took a deep breath.

"Okay," I said. "Here goes nothing."

I opened the bottle of paint thinner Owen had gladly given me when I returned his favorite paintbrush. I dabbed the liquid onto my cotton ball, then began rubbing the corner of the portrait's silver-painted frame. At first, nothing happened. I added a bit more paint thinner and rubbed a little harder.

Then, after a few minutes, the silver paint began to smudge away. Bit by bit. Until a circle of it was completely gone.

Gold glistened underneath.

I dropped my hand and stepped back. The corner of my mouth quirked into a grin. Ricky muttered, "Oh, man!" Bess, George, and Megan simultaneously cheered. Charlotte gasped. I turned to look at her, smiling.

"The treasure," she whispered, hand fluttering to her chest. "It's actually real."

"Yep," I said. "And it's been right here in your house all along!"

Dear Diary,

I WASN'T ABLE TO KEEP MY SORT-OF promise not to get mixed up in a mystery. . . . But we still had an amazing time! Bess, George, and I did get a chance to relax after things settled down. Megan's grand opening went off without a hitch. Even Mr. Plath attended, if you can believe it! He felt bad for giving Megan such a hard time and brought her some early tomatoes from his garden. Judy confessed and will be performing community service and paying restitution for the vandalism and sabotage at Megan's. As for the treasure—even though it technically belongs to Charlotte, she didn't feel right keeping it. She's donated the gold frame to her favorite place: the library. That way, the town can ensure that future generations have access to good books. She's kept the portrait of Elizabeth, though. Because as she told me, being reunited with Judy has reminded her: even when times are difficult, family is the greatest treasure. And you know what? I agree. Family—and good friends—are truly worth their weight in gold!

Which is why, I told Bess and George, our next vacation will be just that. A vacation.

Well, probably . . .

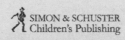